T5-DHC-766

Acclaim *for* the authors of
LIKE MOTHER, LIKE DAUGHTER
(BUT IN A GOOD WAY)

JENNIFER GREENE

"A book by Jennifer Greene hums with an unbeatable combination of sexual chemistry and heartwarming emotion."
> —*New York Times* bestselling author
> Susan Elizabeth Phillips

"A spellbinding storyteller of uncommon brilliance."
> —*Romantic Times BOOKreviews*

NANCY ROBARDS THOMPSON

"Drama and humor make this book hard to put down."
> —*Romantic Times BOOKreviews* on
> *True Confessions of the Stratford Park PTA*

"Top Pick! Told with a captivating voice and clever observations of life's nuances."
> —*Romantic Times BOOKreviews* on
> *Out with the Old, In with the New*

PEGGY WEBB

"Only someone with Peggy Webb's talent could create a read that is both lyrical and irreverent."
> —Charlotte Hughes, *New York Times* bestselling
> author

"With humor, Webb shows that everyone made the best decisions they could at the time but that there's always room for growth."
> —*Romantic Times BOOKreviews* on
> *Flying Lessons*

Jennifer Greene lives near Lake Michigan with her husband and two children. Before writing full-time, she worked as a teacher and a personnel manager. Michigan State University honored her as an "outstanding woman graduate" for her work with women on campus.

Ms. Greene has written more than fifty category romances, for which she has won numerous awards, including two RITA® Awards from the Romance Writers of America and a Career Achievement award from *Romantic Times BOOKreviews*.

Nancy Robards Thompson is a sister, wife and mother who has lived the majority of her life south of the Mason-Dixon line. Upon graduating from college with a degree in journalism, this award-winning author discovered that reporting "just the facts" bored her silly. Since hanging up her press pass to write novels full-time, critics have deemed her books "funny, smart and observant." When she's not writing, she enjoys spending time with her family, reading, hiking and doing yoga.

Peggy Webb and her two chocolate Labs live in a hundred-year-old house not far from the farm where she grew up. "A farm is a wonderful place for dreaming," she says. "I used to sit in the hayloft and dream of being a writer." Now, with two grown children and more than forty-five romance novels to her credit, the former English teacher confesses she's still a hopeless romantic and loves to create the happy endings her readers love so well.

When she isn't writing, she can be found at her piano playing blues and jazz or in one of her gardens planting flowers. Still, Peggy's friends love to sit on her front porch inhaling jasmine from her Angel Garden and celebrating her victories—bestseller lists, writing awards, options for film and audio books.

Like Mother, Like Daughter

(But in a Good Way)

Jennifer Greene

Nancy Robards Thompson

Peggy Webb

LIKE MOTHER, LIKE DAUGHTER (BUT IN A GOOD WAY)

copyright © 2007 by Harlequin Books S.A.

i s b n - 1 3 : 9 7 8 - 0 - 3 7 3 - 8 8 1 3 4 - 5

i s b n - 1 0 :　　0 - 3 7 3 - 8 8 1 3 4 - 7

The publisher acknowledges the copyright holders of the individual works as follows:

BORN IN MY HEART
copyright © 2007 by Alison Hart

BECOMING MY MOTHER, AND OTHER THINGS I LEARNED
FROM JANE AUSTEN
copyright © 2007 by Nancy Robards Thompson

THE LONG DISTANCE MOTHER
copyright © 2007 by Peggy Webb

All rights reserved. Except for use in any review, the reproduction or utilization of this work in whole or in part in any form by any electronic, mechanical or other means, now known or hereafter invented, including xerography, photocopying and recording, or in any information storage or retrieval system, is forbidden without the written permission of the publisher, Harlequin Enterprises Limited, 225 Duncan Mill Road, Don Mills, Ontario, Canada M3B 3K9.

This is a work of fiction. Names, characters, places and incidents are either the product of the author's imagination or are used fictitiously, and any resemblance to actual persons, living or dead, business establishments, events or locales is entirely coincidental.

This edition published by arrangement with Harlequin Books S.A.

® and TM are trademarks of the publisher. Trademarks indicated with ® are registered in the United States Patent and Trademark Office, the Canadian Trade Marks Office and in other countries.

TheNextNovel.com

 HARLEQUIN®

PRINTED IN U.S.A.

If you purchased this book without a cover you should be aware that this book is stolen property. It was reported as "unsold and destroyed" to the publisher, and neither the author nor the publisher has received any payment for this "stripped book."

CONTENTS

BORN IN MY HEART

JENNIFER GREENE

From the Author

Dear Reader,

These days we talk a great deal about building security in children—we worry about our kids' lack of self-esteem, our need to help build their confidence, our desire to have our children feel safe and loved and secure. We all know how much those factors can affect whether our kids succeed in life.

But it's easy to forget that moms have all those problems, too.

I adore kids. (And I have two fabulous ones.) I love every minute of being a mom.... But some of those minutes, I was also scared out of my mind, worried witless that I wasn't a good enough mom, that my failures as a parent could hurt those two young lives I loved so hugely. And if it was that scary for me—a hard-core child lover from the day I was born—I figure it has to be even more challenging for an adoptive mom.

So this story is for all you moms...a bravo to you all!

Jennifer Greene

To My Mom:
Who's strong and brave and loving…
And always an inspiration to me.

In the dark bedroom, a Michigan March wind howling outside, Ann suddenly felt a hand on her shoulder.

She didn't scream—although she sure wanted to.

She needed sex right now like she needed a triple yeast infection. Her work day had been endless. Normally she loved working with troubled kids—the meaner the better—but this particular group of adjudicated urban monsters had brought both weapons and nonstop attitude to the table all afternoon. She was beyond wiped out. She was so tired her body didn't know whether to shriek or sleep.

Jay's quiet hand on her shoulder was typical of her husband. He'd always had that doctor's careful touch. Testing, not demanding. Diagnosing her mood, not pushing.

Right then, even his infernal consideration grated against her nerves. She knew what he wanted, and damn it, she just plain didn't.

There was a time she'd jumped Jay three times a week, and he'd jumped her the other four. Hormones had run sizzling-hot between them for years. They'd never seemed to tire of each other. But then, the obvious thing happened. They grew up. Both of them had busy lives, extraordinarily demanding jobs that stole intensive energy and time, and just possibly, age had become a factor in their sex lives, too…not that Ann admitted to approaching menopause.

She fully realized that menopause was a fact of life, but honest-to-Harry, she just had no time to deal with a bunch of crappy pre-menopausal symptoms. Not now. Maybe she could get around to scheduling it in when she was past fifty, but right now she was only forty-two.

Old enough to feel cranky when Jay wanted sex and she didn't.

Slowly, though, that quiet hand on her shoulder turned into two quiet hands. Jay didn't exactly *push* her into the mattress, but he definitely nudged. It was a smooth, tricky gambler's move designed to make her not notice she was suddenly lying prone on her stomach, right where he wanted her. Silent and sure, those big strong hands of his started kneading all the tense muscles in her neck. Then in her shoulders. Then down her spine. She slept nude, always had—so did he—so it wasn't as if there were any barriers between his hands and her skin.

And suddenly that exasperated *Oh No* in her head seemed to re-translate into a meltdown *Oh Yes*.

Backrubs turned her into putty, always had, probably always would. A cranky mood suddenly turned velvet.

Screaming stress suddenly turned silky. Someone released a greedy moan in the darkness—and it didn't seem to be Jay.

"You've been way overtired," he murmured.

That was like saying the sky was blue. And maybe her hours were long, but Jay had patients calling him 24-7, yet he never complained. Guilt itched her conscience, because they were both over-busy—yet she never seemed to think of initiating a backrub for him first.

Right then, though...she stopped thinking altogether.

In the dark, she didn't have crow's-feet or a thickening middle. She didn't have a job that consumed her a little too much. She didn't have stress or anxiety. In the dark...she was just a woman. Turning rapidly into a puddle of a woman.

Those hands of his could make any woman melt. Long, strong fingers combed into her hair, massaging her scalp, creating shivers and lusty sighs. There went her pride. Who needed it? She heard her hungry moan for more, heard Jay chuckle. All right, so she was pitifully weak...but it wasn't as if she had to hide her character flaws from Jay. He knew every nook and cranny of her body, knew exactly what she couldn't resist. Or didn't want to resist.

She turned, blindly reaching for him, her lips parted to invite his to a private party. A very private party.

The phone rang.

Alarm instantly bucked through her. She immediately recognized the ring—it wasn't Jay's cell or hers, but distinctly the private house landline. And few would call the house phone this late except for a family emergency—or their daughter.

For her, the intimate mood severed faster than a bug bite. She tore free from Jay's arms and twisted behind her for the phone. "Lisa?"

Her daughter's voice gasped a chortle of laughter. "Mom! How'd you know it was me? And darn it, you sound sleepy. If I woke you up, I'll have to shoot myself—"

"Don't be silly, love bug. You know your dad and I always want to hear from you."

"Well, I could have waited. I just got excited about telling you something. But if you're tired, I'll call tomorrow—"

"No, of course not. What's wrong?" She bunched a pillow behind her in the dark, not looking at Jay—but she guessed he'd gone on red alert for the late call the same way she had. They both adored their daughter.

"Nothing's wrong, Mom. I just had some news. Something happened…."

On the bedside table, a trickle of silver gleamed. Half consciously, Ann picked it up. She'd found the treasure at a jeweler last weekend. It was still two months until Mother's Day—and obviously it was silly to buy a Mother's Day present for one's daughter—but Ann couldn't resist. The gift was so perfect, so right, for the mom-daughter relationship she had with Lisa.

The pendant was a solid chunk of sterling on one side, strung on a black silk cord. The back was engraved:

Never Forget For A Single Minute
You Didn't Grow Under My Heart—
But In It.

She hadn't shown the gift to Jay yet, not just because there hadn't been a chance, but because he didn't care about trifles like that. But still....

"I located her, Mom. My mother."

"Pardon?" Ann dropped the bracelet. "I'm sorry, honey, I didn't hear you—"

"I think I found her. My birth mother." When she failed to immediately respond, Lisa zoomed on, "You meant it, didn't you, Mom? I mean, you said a bunch of times that it was totally okay if I started looking for her."

"Of course I meant it," Ann said.

"Well, I was studying for the midterm in chemistry last week. Got so tired I was batty. Couldn't sleep. Couldn't think anymore. So I just started messing around the Internet, using some search engines…"

Jay suddenly switched on his bedside light. She motioned for him to turn it off again. She didn't want a light glaring in her eyes. Not at this hour.

"So you think you found the woman," she said cheerily, annoyed when her voice seemed to come out cheap as tin.

"Well, it's not an absolute-positive yet. But it was pretty interesting. I started by plugging in the name you gave me—you know, Nicole Baker. And the other stuff you'd told me, like that she'd just turned sixteen when she had me. That the whole adoption thing had taken place in the hospital in Rochester Hills…."

"Yes," Ann said. She yanked up the sheet. Then a blanket. It was listening to that howling, growling wind outside that suddenly made her feel chilled and shaky to the bone.

"…Anyway, I got it narrowed down to about seven names a couple nights ago. I thought it was cool then. But yesterday, I got it narrowed down to just two. I guess it's not that unusual a name, even if it's the same birthday, so it may still take a while before I know which of those two for sure. Mom?"

"What?"

"The one woman—she lives right here in Sterling Heights!"

"Really." Sterling Heights was barely a half-hour drive away. Amazingly close, Ann thought.

"Yeah, really. I mean, that doesn't mean it's her. It's not like I contacted her yet—"

"Contact her?" When her daughter fell suddenly silent, Ann realized her voice must have sounded sharper than a rasp. "I just didn't hear you, honey. Did you say you planned to contact her?"

"Well, not this instant. But yeah. When I find some time. I've got a bear of a lit paper coming up. Other stuff going on. Like Doug. Anyway...." Lisa spilled on, sounding like she always did, blithe as bliss. Ann could readily picture her in the cramped dorm room at University of Michigan, pillows stuffed behind her, a box of Oreos in sight, heaped clothes on every surface, her bare toes likely painted some unpredictable color—like aqua or purple. "Honestly, I hadn't thought that far ahead. It was just neat. Getting this close to finding her. Who'd have thought it could be this easy? And you know...I'd wondered."

"I know you did."

"Mom, you're sounding weird. But you and Dad both said that you didn't care if I checked this out."

"We absolutely don't," Ann assured her. She squeezed her eyes closed, flashing back to those conversations, remembering how she'd tried to coach Lisa with careful, thoughtful, cheerful warnings—not counting on finding the woman, not counting on liking her if she did find her, not presuming the woman would be comfortable or happy to suddenly have a life interrupted by what she'd seen once as a mistake. Ann had tried not to dwell on the negative. She was just well aware that Lisa wanted "happy" answers and real life rarely seemed inclined to provide those.

"Well...." Lisa's tone momentarily sounded uncertain, then perked up again. "I guess I better go. I love you to bits." Ann heard a yawn, noisy and huge. Then the sound of girls chattering in the background. "Pass on a hug to Dad, too, okay? And Mom?"

"What, love bug?"

"Is Dad going to be mad if I might have overdrawn just a tiny bit?"

"How tiny?"

A big sigh. "There were these boots, you know? The stores just put out all the spring stuff and my winter boots were a yucky mess. And these were on sale. And I'm not actually sure I'm overdrawn. I think it's down to the pennies. And I'll get my work check next week, but...."

"It's okay, Lise. But call us as soon as you know. Don't sit there with an overdrawn account."

"I don't want Dad to be mad at me."

"Like this has happened in the history of the universe?" Ann didn't roll her eyes, but she could have. Lisa had had Jay wrapped around her little finger, big finger, thumb and any other which-way, from the day they'd brought her home.

"Well...I'd feel awful if he was disappointed in me."

"Part of learning to budget and manage your money is making mistakes. Your dad doesn't expect you to be perfect. Neither do I. But you know what?"

"What?"

"You needed another pair of boots like a hole in the head."

"I *KNOW* that, Mom."

"They were really cute, huh?"

"Honestly, they were fantastic. Smooth like butter. Warm. Tall, you know, so they'd look really good with a calf-length skirt…."

Ann closed her eyes, inhaling the girl talk. This was exactly what she missed so fiercely. The sound of her daughter's voice, babbling on about people and fashion and the silly thing that happened at lunch yesterday and the price of bras. Talking about boots wasn't really talking about boots. It was about the spill of words, the sharing, the enjoying each other.

Eventually, though, Ann could hear the buildup of other voices in her daughter's dorm room and figured she'd better give her an out. "Your dad keeps tapping me on the shoulder. He seems to think we shouldn't feel we have to support the phone company single-handedly. Who knows where men get these ideas?"

"Oh, God. Dad didn't hear me about the boots, did he?"

"No, your dad didn't hear about the boots. Stop worrying. You going to try and make it home in the next couple weeks, hon?"

When they hung up, Ann closed her eyes and tried to swallow the thick clog in her throat. The house had been hollow as an ache since Lisa went off to school. She'd

done the first year at home because she was too attached
to spread her wings.

But this year, Lisa had definitely found her way—which
any mom should have wanted her fledgling offspring to do.
And Ann loved watching her daughter soar, develop real
confidence in herself, start to make all kinds of serious life
decisions. It was just…

She missed her so much. All the little things. The
look of those soft blue eyes, the flyaway blond hair, the
delicate features. The two of them, snuggled under
blankets on the couch in the living room, crying over
some silly chick flick. Shopping for shoes—her daughter's
weakness. Shopping for earrings—her weakness. Bumping
hips in the kitchen when they were baking something
sinful and rich just for fun. Lisa, dissolved into giggles
over some joke. The youthful energy and joy when a ton
of young people filled the house, making messes and
noise. The terror when Lisa was sick and those blue eyes
turned dull. Fighting over books—who got to read certain
bestsellers first. Christmases, with Lisa chasing around the
house, thinking she was hiding presents, still as excited
as a child, and Ann, loving to put together the heaped
gifts under the tree, spending a fortune, not caring,
having a ball creating the holiday.

"Ann?"

She heard Jay's voice, as startling as if he'd shaken her

from a deep sleep. She had no idea how long she'd been sitting in the dark, perched on the edge of the bed. The wind was still howling. The night was still dark. Jay was still lying next to her.

"What's wrong?" Jay asked.

Slowly, Ann climbed back under the covers. Carefully. As if she might break if she moved the wrong way or made too much noise. "She spent too much on a pair of boots and thinks she might be overdrawn," she said lightly.

Jay made a sound. Not a sound of impatience, but something else. "No. I mean something sounded really wrong. Was she ill?"

"No, no, there was nothing like that. Everything's fine."

"If some idiot boy let her down—"

"No, not this time." They both knew how easily Lisa fell in love. How easily and completely she loved. Their daughter would—and had—taken in every stray off the street she ever found, whether it was a dog or cat or a boy. "You realize how late it is? We'll both be wiped out tomorrow. I'll tell you about the call at breakfast."

Ann couldn't talk more right then. She was just too crushingly tired, yet the weirdest thing happened when she closed her eyes. Every muscle in her body tensed up as if bracing for a blow.

She couldn't lose the feeling, couldn't shake it. It couldn't be a panic attack, because she was too sturdy and sensible to even imagine suffering a panic attack. And it certainly couldn't be fear wrapping her up in an invisible cloak of ice. She was right *THERE*, in her own bed, Jay next to her, cuddled in an indulgently luxurious down comforter, thriving in her life and work and everything else. What in Sam Hill was there to be afraid of?

Yet it wasn't that kind of blow her body seemed braced for.

It was more like…a tsunami of loneliness. She had the crazy feeling that if she breathed wrong, if she moved from this exact position—like when she was a child and was careful not to step on a sidewalk crack—she could become engulfed, out of control, in a wild emotional wave where no one could hear or save her.

"Ann." Jay's voice, quiet as a murmur, reached out in the darkness. "Whatever it is, we'll find a way to deal with it."

"Of course we will," Ann said.

JAY FLICKED ON THE COFFEEMAKER and hovered, like a jockey at the Derby, for the gates to open and the coffee to surge out. Above his head, he could hear the sounds of Ann stirring…the soft plop of her feet climbing out of bed, then her exuberant race for the bathroom.

He glanced at his watch. If there was anyone to bet with, he'd wager that Ann would be downstairs—fully dressed, war paint on, her thick dark hair miraculously tamed—in sixteen minutes flat.

He'd finished the first mug of coffee, checked his office messages, half read the paper and had the car keys on the table when she flew down the stairs.

"Morning," she said, and honed in on the coffee machine like a rabid dog for fresh prey.

"Morning." His mind flashed on an old memory. Not their wedding day, not the first day they met…but the first morning they woke up together. An earth goddess, he'd thought, with all that wild dark hair and slumberous dark eyes and soft, full curves. He'd slept around a ton more than she had, but she'd been the one to teach him about sex— about feeling, about inciting, about giving. About how the right woman could turn a guy inside out and open up his whole damn life.

He'd never felt certain that he'd done the same and opened hers. "Did you sleep okay?" he asked her.

"Just fine. You?"

"You ever know me to have a problem sleeping?"

She chuckled, bussed him on the head and started whirling around the kitchen like a gypsy dervish. Last year, she'd had the counters and floors done in granite and tile, and when the terrorizing re-dec horror was over, he thought the kitchen looked more like her. Sturdy. Bright. Everything in its place, easy upkeep. Attractive enough—but nothing was going to penetrate that crusty protective surface unless she let it happen.

He'd always had to struggle to read her. This morning, he searched hard for clues, trying to fathom why the call from Lisa last night had upset her so much, but nothing jumped out at him. The rust sweater and camel hair skirt were favorites of hers, clothes she picked when she was expecting a rough day. She was sentimental that way, always had been. She wore a necklace and earrings, copper disks, dangling stuff—Ann liked her jewelry, but she tended toward bohemian, playful pieces, nothing expensive.

Jay always figured it was because she didn't want people to think she was vain. Jewelry wasn't about adornment; it was about fun. Nothing he'd ever said had convinced that woman that she was beautiful. He thought it was partly because she never studied herself in a mirror when she was smiling or being herself. She was always looking for flaws, so naturally the mirror gave them back to her.

This morning, it didn't take a mirror to reveal the smudges under her eyes from lack of sleep, her darting-around nerves.

"How's your schedule?" she asked him.

"Two surgeries this morning. Neither a big deal. And then just hospital visits this afternoon. An easy day."

"In other words," Ann spoke with the knowledge of a doctor's wife, "you'll be lucky if the spare emergencies let you get home before six."

"That'd be my guess, too. Your day?"

"I've got a meeting at 8:15. And I might be a couple minutes late, but even a tyrant couldn't expect me to show up without coffee…" She lifted her mug. "God, this is good. How come you make so much better coffee than me?"

"Because I'm so handsome."

"Yeah. That must be it. Anyway. Three hellions this morning—one of them a girl. It's so easy to say, 'kick them out of school,' but the question is…then what? Granted, the hard core ones are nothing but a pain in a classroom setting. But they're already throwaways. What are we supposed to do, just let them sit home and cause crime?"

"No," he said firmly.

She blinked at him, obviously unsure what the connection was. "No what?"

"No bringing any more throwaways home."

"Jay! I haven't brought home a kid in ages!"

"Yeah, but you're always thinking about it." Lonesome eyes tracked her smile, but she was quickly grabbing her keys, her work cell, her car-coffee-mug, her sunglasses.

"Dry cleaning to pick up tonight."

"You want me to do it?"

"No. My turn. But I want you to tackle that idiot at the electric company about the bill. Tonight. No more waiting."

"Okay."

"I taped some movie on TiVo last night. Can't remember what. But if we have time—"

"Good."

She was gone. Just like that. He should have aimed out the driveway with her—he was already five minutes late himself, and Jay didn't do late. Instead, he stood there in the milky east light for another few moments, waiting for the sharp crack in his chest to stop hurting.

She'd kissed him good morning. Kissed him goodbye. But she hadn't seen him.

They'd been in the middle of making love last night. Good love. Hot love—if he said so himself. The phone call had naturally interrupted their mood, nothing odd about that. But once the call came in, she'd completely forgotten him as if he didn't exist. She'd not only forgotten about making love. She'd forgotten him.

Jay tried to remember back to when he'd had a wife.

He locked the door, feeling the spanking slap of icy morning air as he climbed into the seven-year-old Mercedes. Ann kept pushing him to trade the baby in, but she was still good as gold. Black, sleek and quiet. The radio was automatically tuned to NPR, the seat adjusted for his long legs and the M.D. plates guaranteed the cops would let him slide if he was speeding.

More relevant, the car knew its way to the hospital without his having to think. And right then, he couldn't help remembering how he'd almost lost Ann when she'd discovered her infertility. She'd barreled into a depression so hard, so deep, so heartbreaking, that damn it, he'd been afraid he really would lose her. Ann loved kids. Loved people. Hell, Ann had more love in her than a hundred ordinary people—but she so wanted children of her own.

And then they'd adopted Lisa, and they'd been okay.

At least mostly okay. He'd lost his wife. Lisa became the sun and the world to her. But Ann had come alive again, returned to her pumped-up vibrant self. She'd poured herself into the home and their family, always thinking of everyone's needs but her own—even after she'd started working with troubled kids again. Even after she'd gone back for her Master's degree so she could really tackle the hellion-aged misfits. But nothing mattered more to her than Lisa.

He fit in there somewhere. Jay knew that. She'd just stopped…looking at him. He was in her life like a faucet or a light switch. A fixture.

Sometimes he wasn't dead sure she knew who she was sleeping with. Jay had no worries that she wasn't physically satisfied. Hormones ran paler than they used to, but Ann still had plenty of heat, plenty of need, plenty of plain old earthy lust in her. Which she still willingly released on him…but only when he initiated sex.

She never initiated it herself anymore.

He thought…hoped…that when Lisa went off to school, he might just get his Ann back. Now, that seemed foolish. All the couples around them had cooled their marriage jets.

The ones still together seemed attached like bungee cords, pulled together for crises, pulled away by the rest of their lives—the parts of their lives that really engaged their time and energy and emotion. The men had their work. The women had their work.

It was pretty embarrassing to still be in love with your wife when no one else seemed to feel that way anymore. Marriage was just marriage. Better than being single five million times over. But…everybody was a long time past the era when you couldn't survive three nights without screwing, when you craved getting home from work so you could be with the other person. Your mate could hurt your feelings deeper and faster than anyone else, could make you feel better deeper and faster than anyone else.

That's how it used to be. But nobody expected it to still be like that after twenty years.

Jay didn't like feeling like a fool.

He tried to force his mind on the gall bladder surgery he had scheduled that morning. And did.

But before he turned into the hospital parking lot, he was reminded that Ann hadn't said a word about the call from Lisa last night. Something in that call had clearly shaken her. He hadn't overheard her say anything telling to their daughter, but he'd seen her posture, felt her anxiety long after the call was over.

He knew better than to push.

Pushing Ann had the same effect as a hammer on a mountain. Nothing budged.

But for damn sure—soon—he needed to find out what had been said in that conversation.

CHAPTER 2

A book hurled through the air. Then came an angry flutter of papers.

Ann stood, as calm and motionless as she could with her heart pounding like a freight train, while the teenager vented more rage.

The sixteen year old was out of control, no question about that. She skidded a student desk across the floor, causing it to crash into a bookcase. Then swept an entire windowsill shelf of books crashing down. It was all Ann could do not to flinch—but that was the only thing she swore not to do, because it was the one thing the kid was expecting.

Rose Marie had wild scoops of brunette curls, a terrific figure, three facial rings, two tattoos with boys' names and a model-pretty face. She'd have been downright breathtaking except for the angry eyes. At least they weren't dead eyes, though, Ann mused. The anger was as clear and bright as fire. And all that fierce, violent anger gave Ann hope that there was still a kid in there, trying to find a way to cope with problems way beyond her realm.

"You think you can keep me here? Nobody can keep me anywhere! And you're as full of shit as everybody else!"

"I'm not trying to keep you anywhere, Rose," Ann said quietly. "You have a choice—to either be here with me or go back to lock up."

"You think I care? Like there's a big difference between juvie and here. Besides, I don't care if I'm here, anyway. You can't make me do anything. I'd like to see you try. Go on. Try. Stop me."

She lifted another chair over her head. Crashed it. The dent in the drywall made Ann mentally cringe. She was pretty handy with a hammer and a screwdriver, could even tackle a power tool now and then. She'd learned to, because Jay wasn't exactly the most mechanical guy in town. But drywall…yuck. She could probably do it, because—after all—a woman could do anything if she had to. But basically, there were times when women's lib was still alive and thriving, and other moments when it was just a whole lot easier to throw in the towel and hire a guy.

"STOP me!" Rose Marie taunted again.

Ann had already considered doing just that—because it mattered, whether the teenager would wind down after venting some anger, or whether all that destruction and violence could accelerate. If Ann had misjudged and Rose couldn't start quieting down, they were potentially aimed for disaster, because Ann was three inches shorter and a good twenty pounds lighter than the teenager. Not to mention a tad older.

Rose Marie lifted another chair, looked at Ann, and then gave it an exasperated push instead of throwing it. "Whatsa *MATTER* with you? You don't even talk. You just stand there and do nothing. What kind of counselor are you, anyway?"

Ann didn't say "your last chance." Hells bells, that would probably have started another rampage. "I'm the kind of counselor who's going to teach you to read," she said.

"I told you! I can read! I can read any time I want to! This is so stupid!" As if frustrated beyond all sanity, the teenager threw herself in a corner and sank to the ground.

Ann pushed away from the desk then and slowly approached her. Not too close. Just close enough to be able to talk without either of them raising their voices. "You've been in and out of juvie since you were eleven, Rose. Petty theft. Vandalism. Fights. Every kind of trouble you could find to get into—except for drugs. And you know what that tells me?"

"Like I care what that tells you?"

"It tells me that you've still got some hope that something good can happen to you. That's why you haven't chosen the drug route, at least yet. You're still fighting for your life."

"That's total crap."

"You've got no way to climb out of the messes you're

in if you can't read. So that's where it has to start. Sitting down, doing the hard work of learning to read from the beginning—"

"You don't know me. You don't know whether I can read or not. You don't know anything about me—"

"I know the system's been trying to throw you away from third grade on. Everybody wants you to disappear, Rose, because no one can seem to figure out what to do with you. Including you. But this is the deal. The buck stops here. You're stuck with me because I'm not about to throw you away. Once we've figured out this reading thing, THEN you can throw me out if you want. But until that time…it's me or jail, girl. Your choice."

Rose Marie seemed to think about that for a minute. Then she surged to her feet, picked up another chair and hurled it at the wall.

Ann mentally sighed. Her boss claimed Ann had an amazing gift for reaching impossible-to-reach teenagers— that she was one of the few people who could actually get blood out of a turnip. Ann loved that kind of praise. Some days she even thought it was true.

But some days, like this one, it didn't pay to get out of bed.

By the time she pulled in her driveway at home, it was past five, and all she wanted was a long, hot soak, a glass of Pinot Noir and some Chinese takeout. Her mood clunked another notch when she walked in. The silence in the empty house was heavier than gloom. She pushed off her shoes, snapped on the kitchen light and spotted the answering machine blinking.

It was Jay. "I tried to reach you on your cell, but you must have turned it off. Figured you were with one of your hellions. Hope it went well. I've got a pregnant patient with a ruptured spleen. Car accident. Right now the chances look slim that I'll make it home before midnight. You know you can reach me if you need to."

Okay. So this was going to be a solo night. She poked around the fridge, looking for the half open bottle of Pinot Noir, thinking that Jay was going to be exhausted when he finally got home. And it would kill him if he lost a patient. Especially a pregnant patient.

She was just pouring a glass when a sudden rap on the back door made her spill it. There was no reason to expect any kind of interruption, not at home and at this hour—but then a flyaway blond head poked in the door.

"Hey, Mom!"

"*LISE!*" Ann jammed the glass on the counter and charged across the room. God. She squeezed until Lisa squealed, but she couldn't help it. Nothing, absolutely nothing, smelled or felt or sounded as good as having her daughter this close. "How come you didn't call? I'd have had dinner ready if I'd known you were coming—"

"I got a ride. John. One of the guys in the dorm. He's

going to drive me back to school, too, so I only have a couple hours, but I thought hey, why not?"

Exhaustion flew out the door. Discouragement, frustration, loneliness, sore feet—and every other complaint Ann had about the day—flew out the door, too.

"Have you already had dinner?" Lisa asked. "Any chance you're hungry?"

"Starved." Actually, she hadn't been, but she was now. She handed Lisa the car keys. "You pick the place, whatever you want. When do you have to be back?"

"By eight, eight-thirty latest. Where's Dad?"

"He's stuck at the hospital, I'm afraid. He's going to be mighty unhappy he missed you." Naturally, Lisa's choice was Red Lobster. Lisa might have thought there was a question, but Ann knew better.

Conversation bubbled over from the drive to the time they were seated, the place already filling up with a buzz of people. "So those are the boots, huh?"

"Yup. Aren't they adorable?" Lisa immediately stuck out her long skinny legs, showing off the jean skirt, that top that skimmed her navel and showed off her nonexistent chest. God, she was cute. "Dad called me about these boots, you know."

"He did?" Jay hadn't mentioned it.

"Yeah. You remember the night I called you last week? Well, it was like the day after. Dad called, gave me a big talk about balancing checkbooks and credit cards and all that. Oh, and about overdrawing. Then he said I could buy another pair of boots if I wanted. But only if I'd be really careful not to do that again."

"So…you wrapped him around your finger again."

"Mom! I didn't ask him to buy me another pair of boots! Oh my GOD this is good." Lisa was diving into the mashed potatoes and cheddar biscuits, even before she'd gotten into the crab.

"How you can stay skinny as a rail is beyond me."

"I figure it's metabolism. Either that or I'm really a pig at heart." Her eyes were dancing devilment—even as she reached for another muffin and lavishly buttered it. "You were right about U of M, you know."

"About what?"

"I have to admit, it really is on the dark side. Heavy on the politics." Lisa sighed. "I'm finding my place and all. Good friends. Good classes. At least some of them. But man. It wouldn't kill people to smile when you walk down the street. And everybody's so about their cause."

Ann had been so afraid the school, no matter how terrific its reputation, would eat up her baby.

"Hey…." Halfway through the crab, Lisa suddenly looked up. Both of them had flushed cheeks and messy hands. "Almost forgot to tell you. I met her."

Ann didn't ask who "her" was. She'd convinced herself for

days there wasn't an elephant in the living room. Hadn't told Jay. Hadn't asked Lisa anything further in their last week of conversations. Yet now, that thick slug in her stomach recognized immediately who Lisa was talking about.

"Tell me all about it," she said casually. She put down her fork, wiped her hands.

"Well...she was the Nicole in Sterling Heights. In fact, that was the thing, Mom. When John offered me the ride home, that was my chance to meet her face-to-face this afternoon. I almost didn't tell you." Lisa looked up, peered into her eyes. "If you had any problem with my doing this, I wouldn't have. I'd die a zillion times over before hurting you."

"Lisa, it's perfectly okay. Why would I be hurt? I always understood why you'd be curious about her."

Lisa heaved a sigh, and then dove straight back into the crab with no holds barred. "That's exactly the thing. I just wanted to know. No one could ever possibly take your place. I know you know that. I just couldn't stop wondering what my birth mother looked like. What she WAS like. Whether she loved the guy she slept with who was my dad. What happened."

"Uh-huh."

"The other woman—remember, there were two I was looking into? She turned out to be half Spanish. Very pretty lady, but obviously—" Lisa pointed a butter-dripping finger at her face, the blond hair, the pale skin "—it just doesn't seem remotely likely I could ever have any Mexican blood."

"I'd say the chances were a million to one," Ann agreed. The tables around them had packed in. It was one of those all-you-could-eat-crab nights. The room had become warm, redolent with the smells of seafood and butter, the music of voices, the occasional clatter of plates. A child laughed. Outside, night was coming on fast.

"So, anyway, it had to be the Nicole in Sterling Heights. Or I thought it had to be. All the clues pointed there. So I called. And she agreed to meet me sometime. I thought, over spring break or summer, but when John offered that ride today, I just took a chance, called to see if it'd work for her...." Lisa suddenly lifted a fork in the air. "Man, I am so stuffed."

"Where's the surprise? You packed away enough to feed a cow."

Lisa giggled. "I know. It's not my fault. I'm insane crazy for crab."

"I know you are." But it kept echoing in Ann's mind how Lisa had just met her birth mother that afternoon. Just hours ago. And before seeing her, before coming home. In fact, obviously she wouldn't likely have come home if it wasn't for the chance to be with her birth mother.

"I'll be napping the whole ride back to school. Anyway...Mom, she's beautiful. Thirty-five, but she doesn't look over thirty. Nice house. Not nice like ours, but it's still okay. She's married, I guess for the second time. Two kids, but they were both in school, not there. In fact, nobody was around but the two of us. She does some kind of photography part time."

Plates were taken away. Hands cleaned. Lisa made a run for the restroom. The waitress brought out the selection of desserts. Lisa wanted one so badly she was salivating, but couldn't decide because she was so full.

Ann had the eerie sensation that she was a robot in an animated movie. Everyone was moving but her, everyone alive but her. She was smiling, she thought. And looking attentive—she hoped. But dinner had settled in her stomach in one big, heavy clunk.

"Anyway..." Lisa came back from the restroom and grabbed a spoon for the double-chocolate confection in front of her, which Ann had ordered for her without needing to think. She'd always been able to guess what Lisa wanted before her daughter even knew, and they were running out of time to finish dinner and get home before Lisa's ride got there.

"Anyway," Lisa repeated, "Nicole invited me to come see her again. Whenever I could. She really meant it, Mom. You know, you read these stories, about how the birth kid shows up and interrupts the poor woman's life, like an embarrassing secret she was trying to hide? Only Nicole was nothing like that. She wants me to meet her husband. And my half sisters. Imagine! I have half sisters! Is that a giant wow or what?"

"I'll say it's a giant wow," Ann agreed heartily. "Honey,

it's past seven-thirty, we've got to get the check and hustle, if your ride's going to be at the house by eight."

"Oh, damn. I was hoping to have enough time to get some stuff from my closet!"

"What do you need? I can bring it up to school."

"No, I'm just being silly. I wanted to stash my heavy parka at home and bring up a sweatshirt and spring jacket, but really, it's dumb. It's still freezing, for Pete's sake. And I'll be home for spring break in ten days…"

When they got home, Jay was just pulling in the drive. The instant Lisa spotted him, she flew from the car like a bird. "Dad! I was so afraid I wouldn't get a chance to see you!"

"You almost didn't, I was afraid I was going to be hung up all night at the hospital. I'm going to take a wild guess that you two have been to Red Lobster?"

"How'd you know?"

Ann stood back, loving watching the two of them together. Many times, she and Jay had accused each other of spoiling Lisa. Both knew it was true. Both tried to get tougher, but it was hard. Lisa was so loving, so happy and giving by nature. And how could you spoil a child with too much love?

Still, where Ann never doubted Jay loved their daughter 100 percent, there was a difference in how Ann felt for her. Lisa was a corner of her soul, the core of her heart. Partly she felt that way because it was the only child she'd ever have. Partly because it was a daughter. And partly because

Lisa was Lisa. Whatever the combination of reasons, Ann felt, deep down, that she'd never survive if something happened to her daughter.

Another car pulled in the driveway—from the look of its decrepit condition, it likely belonged to John, Lisa's college friend. The lanky kid who climbed out had a wild orange afro, more freckles than face and was shivering inside a very trendy, very inadequate light jacket.

"So anyway, Dad, Mom'll tell you all about meeting my birth mother, Nicole. She probably told you about it all before. Have you guys met John?"

Ann had to grin—the first natural grin she'd felt for hours—just seeing Jay respond to the boy. Poor Jay, he was so protective. Clearly the kid was just a friend—a conclusion Ann reached not just because the in-guy this month was Doug, but because the kids showed no connection at all. Still, Jay looked the boy over as if he were a piece of meat appropriate for skewering on a barbecue.

Then, it was all confusion, with more kisses and hugs, car doors slamming, Lisa talking at the same time as Ann—which they always did. Lisa's hair flew every which way as she tucked in the front seat of the old relic, and finally their car lights backed out of the driveway.

Jay stood with his hands on his hips and a scowl. "You think that rust heap'll make it to Ann Arbor?"

"It's only an hour's drive or so."

"That's why I'm asking. It doesn't look as if it could make it two blocks." He shot her a wry look and lifted an arm—their old signal for her to edge up against his side for a hug—and they walked that way into the house. Of course they separated immediately then. Jay disappeared to hang up his coat. Ann tossed her purse, turned on lights.

"I was afraid you'd be much later," she said.

"So was I. Thought I was going to lose the girl for sure. The baby's still a question, but he's holding his own, under the pediatrician's care now. And the little mom is one wiped-out puppy, but looks like she's on the recovery track." Jay opened the refrigerator.

"I'll make you something. I was beat when I first came home—but still, I can't be half as tired as you must be."

"I can just build a sandwich. Not that hungry."

Yeah, well, Jay always said that. He even meant it. But if she put decent food in front of him, he'd level it. And although Ann resented always being the assigned cook just because she was female, fact was, both of them had heavy work schedules and needed serious nutrition to maintain their hectic pace.

Eventually they drifted toward the den, Jay carrying a plate, Ann drawing curtains and turning on the tube. Without Lisa at home, the den had become their evening cocoon, eating in here in front of the TV, with their books and "stuff" all around them.

Originally Ann thought the room looked tasteful and kind of elegant, with leather chairs, French blue walls and crown molding, but then....well, life happened to it. The floor-to-ceiling bookcases were untidily jammed with all sizes and kinds of reading material. The glass on the coffee table hadn't been visible in years because of books and magazines, yarn and puzzles, photos—all the stuff that had no place and someone actually wanted to get to, but there just never seemed the time to do it.

They listened to headline news, but then Jay, who suffered panic attacks without the remote in his hand—switched to TiVo. "Old movie or new?"

"Hmm. The old Hitchcock sounds like a good way to relax tonight. We've both had an extra long day."

"You're not kidding." He was sitting in the butternut leather chair next to her, and clicked on the movie—but then stopped it. "Why didn't you tell me Lisa was searching for her birth mother?"

Ann leaned forward, shuffled through the magazines and catalogs for something to go mindless with. "It wasn't news. She told us both she was going to do it."

"Ann."

She heard the patience in his voice. It made her want to smack him. Not REALLY smack him, since neither of them would hit a fly and certainly never each other. But she just didn't like being pushed. And never by him. "Lisa just met the woman this afternoon. I had no idea that was going to happen—and I don't think she did either—until the actual meeting. Which she came right home to tell us about."

Jay fell silent. She didn't look at him. She looked at the Soft Surroundings catalog, and then Norm Thompson.

Still, he didn't start the movie. Finally he tried another direction of conversation. "So that's what her call was about the other night. Not new boots and whether she was overdrawn. But that she was doing the birth mom search."

"She mentioned it then, yes." Ann spotted a skirt she loved on sight. It was one of those fashion statements that she couldn't possibly wear without looking like an elephant. But man, it was so sensuous and silky looking. The kind of thing she could wear in her imagination.

Again Jay fell silent. Again he finally spoke up. "If this is going to hurt you, I'll speak to Lisa. I'm certain she would stop if she thought it would trouble you—"

"Please. Do NOT speak to Lisa." She slipped the catalog under the nest on the table. That's exactly why she couldn't throw things out—because she still wanted things even when she knew she couldn't or shouldn't have them. "We both told Lisa we were okay with her doing this. I meant it. So did you."

"But the circumstances suddenly completely changed if she actually found the woman."

"Not really," Ann said. "We can't stop her, Jay. I don't

want her to think we're insecure about her loving us or our loving her. She has every right to figure out what role this woman could or might have in her life. Or who she is, in any sense. It's part of her identity. Part of the questions kids are supposed to ask themselves when they're in college. They're looking for who they are. This woman is part of that equation for Lisa."

"That sounds very wise. But it's also theory. In reality, I have to believe you're upset—"

"I'm not remotely upset. It was all very interesting."

"Uh-huh," Jay said.

She heard that patient tone of his again and gave him a good, long glare. "Would you switch on the movie?"

"Okay," he said. And did. Ann reached for the down throw behind the chair to cuddle up with. *Psycho*. It was just what she needed. Something terrorizing and gruesome to distract her mind.

And her heart.

On Saturday mornings, Jay hit the hospital early, checked on his recovery patients before ten if he could, so he'd have the rest of the day free. This particular Saturday, when he left the house, Ann had been sleeping and the house was quiet as a secret.

When he walked back in, the whole house was in a complete uproar. Ann, flush-cheeked and exuberant, was boogying around the kitchen singing godawful old rock and roll. Bags of groceries blocked the whole kitchen table surface. A cake was baking in the oven, judging from the fabulous smell. The sink area was cluttered with blueberries and nectarines—out of season. The far counter was clogged with enough soda to sink a ship, particularly Dr Pepper, and every snack known to man. Especially chocolate.

Before taking off his jacket, he fingered through the chocolate heap for Hershey's Special Dark. Every man needed a vice, as far as Jay was concerned. Or five.

Ann whirled around and spotted him. He got a kiss on a cheek—faster than lightning, and not enough to stop her from singing the old Revolution lyrics—and then came the questions. "Did you put gas in the car?"

"And washed it." He motioned tactfully at all the chaos. "You know, the last I remember, except for crab, she barely eats enough to keep a bird alive."

"I know, I know. But I still like to have her favorites around."

Man, he didn't want to rain on her parade. She was so happy. And Ann, happy, was the best aphrodisiac he'd ever seen. Just being around that smile was infectious for everyone around her. But it was hard not to worry when someone was that high. "You know, honey, she isn't going to be home every single day. It's just spring break—"

"I know. Honestly. In fact, she said a lot of her friends were going on trips. Just like her to be working this week instead of playing, isn't it? Anyway…I just thought I'd better have food around. You know how she likes to have people over…."

Jay knew how Ann liked to have the house full. And how Ann was hoping their daughter would spend every minute at home. She turned to him again, this time with her eyes filled with tears. Not sad tears. She was slicing thin onions for barbecued ribs. Lisa's favorite.

"You want me to do that?"

"God, yes." She cheerfully handed him the knife. "You're the surgeon."

Not for onions, but whatever. "You know," he said again

cautiously, "She's only an hour away. It's not like she's been in Siberia…."

"You don't need to tell me I'm being perfectly silly! I know! And all week, I told myself I wouldn't go so crazy this time." Ann shook her head at all the messes. "Now look at me."

"Well….it's logical. We just plain miss her."

"Exactly." A beam of a smile, just for him this time. "And I just want things right, you know? Easy. So if all the food's in the house and everything's done, then when she's got time to be with us, there's no fuss. It's all done." Her brow furrowed for a sudden flash of alarm. "Good grief, I have to run upstairs and close her window. I just opened it a few minutes, so there'd be fresh air up there, but I don't want it freezing—did you see the daffodils peeking up in the backyard? She's coming home at the perfect time…."

Ann disappeared up the stairs, still talking as if he could hear her. Jay ducked down to his slicing onions job and damn near sliced off his finger. With a scalpel, he was king. Why was a cleaver so different?

He was near the end of the job—his eyes tearing like fire—when the phone rang. He had to cradle the receiver between his shoulder and ear to keep on with the knife at the same time.

"Dad!" Lisa's voice had the lilt of laughter. "First time I've caught you first in forever! Listen, though, I told Mom I'd be home around lunch, but I just talked to Nicole. She asked me to come over. She's been working up to telling her two kids about me, and that's the thing, she thought this would be a good time for me to meet them. We're just going to a park for a couple hours, nothing long, just a low-key thing. I just want to meet my half sisters, you know? I'd still be home before dinner, if that's okay."

Jay frowned, looking at the messes strewn in every direction. "Well, normally, that'd be fine, honey, but your mom's really counting on your coming home. If there's another day you could do that—"

"Is that Lisa?" Ann bounded down the stairs with a smile bigger than sunshine and grabbed the phone. "Hey, baby, are you on your way?"

Jay stood helpless. It was like watching a puppy get kicked. Originally that smile of anticipation and love took up Ann's whole face, lighting up her skin, her eyes, the energy glowing off her. The more she listened to Lisa's conversation, the more that smile softened, and finally changed to such a fiercely disappointed expression that it was kin to pain.

But that's not what showed up in the conversation Lisa heard.

"Of course it's all right, you silly," she said to their daughter. "How could you not want to meet your half sisters? Take your camera, okay, so you can take some pictures and show us what they look like. We'll just see you when we see you…no, no, honey, this is *home*, you don't have to worry about any kind of schedule with us…."

When Ann hung up the phone, she stood there for a second or two, as if suspended in time. When she turned around, she was that other woman. The woman he didn't know. Not his wife, but the woman who'd showed up in his life and bed years ago and refused to leave the house, yet didn't seem to see him or relate to him.

She was still smiling, but it was like a Crayola drawing. The eyes didn't meet his. The zoom had gone out of her posture. "Well," she said, "Lisa'll be later than we thought."

Jay couldn't remember feeling so damned helpless. He wasn't used to feeling lost. At the hospital, people turned to him with life or death issues that he readily took on, the ethics, the responsibility, the action. Yet with Ann...he didn't have a clue what to say or do.

It was just so clear that everything she wanted to do that day had gone completely down the drain. God knew, he didn't even enter the equation.

"You know, if we've got the early afternoon free...we could go to a movie," he said.

She chuckled, but there was no humor in it. "Actually, we can't. I've got a cake coming out of the oven—sponge cake—need to make marshmallow frosting for it. All this food to put away. And I still have to put in the ribs, they're all defrosted."

"We could still duck out of the house for a couple hours. Catch some fresh air—"

But no, there was a reason she couldn't do that either. She didn't want to be tired when Lisa finally did get home. And if they didn't go low key now, she'd never be able to stay up that night.

Jay was fairly sure—not completely sure—but fairly sure that Ann didn't mean to reject him. Her choices were about Lisa. It was perfectly natural that both of them missed their daughter, wanted to focus time on her when she was finally home. Right?

Right, he told himself. And had been telling himself.

And still wanted to tell himself.

But more and more, he felt invisible in Ann's life. He still loved her, still yearned for her, still cherished her. But he wasn't damn sure she'd miss him if he disappeared for a few weeks…or even if she'd notice.

It wasn't a situation he could live with forever.

LATER THAT EVENING, Ann sank on the couch in the den, feeling buoyant as a bubble. The ribs had been way overcooked, but that hadn't hurt them. Lisa had inhaled the sponge cake with marshmallow frosting. And ten minutes after arrival, the hall and living room and kitchen were a mess of clothes and belongings and stuff—the same teenage crap Ann had yelled at her about cleaning up all those years—but now just made her feel plain old happy to see.

Their daughter bounced into the den, having changed

from jeans to what she called home clothes: sweats that the Salvation Army would have rejected, bare feet, an oversized sweatshirt of Jay's that she'd kidnapped years before and still hung on her like a trash bag over a stick.

"You ready for a movie?" Ann asked.

Jay groaned, provoking Lisa to laugh and bend down to kiss her father. "You afraid we're going to watch a chick flick, aren't you, Dad?"

"I'm afraid to answer that on the grounds that it might incriminate me," he said. "But you two can watch whatever you want. I'll suffer in silence."

"Now you know you'll fall asleep as soon as we get to a kiss scene, so you won't have to suffer THAT long," Lisa teased. Like the old days, she curled up on the couch next to Ann and pulled the old down throw over both of them. She couldn't watch a movie without a blankie. Come to think of it, neither could Ann.

"Bunch of kids asked me to go to a movie, but I told 'em no. I just really wanted an evening at home with you two," Lisa said. "But before we start a movie…let's catch up on all the family news. Especially on my cousins. Who's in trouble? Who's in disgrace?"

Ann could see Jay rolling his eyes behind his newspaper. The movie they'd seen five million times, Jay teasing about their "girl" choices and the catch-up chitchat after dinner…it was all as familiar as roses in summer. So was the family gossip.

Ann had two older sisters, both of whom had three kids each. Everyone had children but Ann, which—until they'd adopted Lisa—had hurt like a raw sore. She'd always felt like…less. Less important, less of a human being. And for darn sure, less of a woman.

"Mom?" Lisa prompted when Ann didn't immediately regale her with the latest family stories. "What happened with Bob and that girl? The one who got pregnant? And then, last time we talked about Jodi, Aunt Becca thought she was into drugs. And what's Grandma been saying about all this?"

"Your grandmother," Jay said from behind his newspaper, "will have been telling your mother in every phone call that she's the only one who knows how to raise children, because you turned out perfect."

"I should call Grandma and tell her how smart she is," Lisa said thoughtfully.

Jay, predictably, whacked her over the head with the *Journal*.

Ann opened her mouth, wanting to join in the teasing, yet suddenly pulled back. It never occurred to her before how often she'd chatted about the family "kid" problems. For absolutely certain she'd never found pleasure in her sisters' woes or trouble with their children. She adored her nieces and her sisters both, would have done anything for them. But it *had* turned into a little family game. Dishing the family dirt.

She could remember—too damn well—when she was

the subject of family discussions. Her mom and sisters would huddle in the kitchen during family dinners, gently singing the same old tune, wasn't it a shame Ann couldn't have children, how she was missing so much, how sad it all was. She always knew the family meant to be empathetic…but somehow she'd always felt so inadequate and incompetent and incomplete. Like a failure as a woman.

Until she'd had Lisa.

"Mom, what's wrong? You have the weirdest expression."

Ann lifted a hand. "I was just thinking…how I used to feel like an outsider. An imposter in the family. As if everyone had a place at the table but me." When Jay and Lisa looked at her blankly, she chuckled. "Okay, forget it. I just had a nuts moment, that's all. Say, did you bring some pictures of Nicole's two children?"

"Yup. You sure you want to see them?" Lisa queried.

Jay started to say—"Didn't you two want to watch a movie?"—but Ann interrupted and said what had to be said. "Of course we do."

Lisa searched through the leather contraption she called a purse and came up with a half-dozen photos. "Nicole took these with a digital camera cuz she didn't actually have prints around. We just made them from her printer. You can tell she's a photographer, though, can't you? This was just from their last Christmas. And a couple from a skiing trip they all took together last month…."

Jay lurched out of his chair and perched on the couch arm, making it easy for both of them to see the photos at the same time. She felt his hand on her back, not rubbing exactly, yet kind of absently kneading the nape of her neck. She wasn't sure why. She wasn't tense.

At least...she wasn't tense exactly.

Or for any good reason.

The two little girls were not only adorable. They looked just like Lisa used to. Blond fairies, with a halo of spun silk around pale faces, big blue eyes, skinny legs.

"This one is Samantha. Sammie. She's almost eleven. She's the athletic one by far. I guess Nicole was only married to her dad for a little while. Anyway, she really got off on the idea of a sudden big sister...but then it was kind of hard. She didn't know what to say. Neither did I. I mean, I wasn't going to ask her the usual, what grade are you in school and that kind of lame stuff, you know? But I think it'll just take some time being with her before she can get comfortable. And this one..."

Lisa, going into full bubble mode now, wound her legs up and handed them the next photo. "See the little one? She's just eight. Emily..."

Again Ann felt Jay's hand on her back. Warm. Heavy. Distracting.

"What a love," Ann said.

"Oh, she *is*, Mom. A girl's girl, all the way. Little

magnetic earrings. And socks with fluffy edges. And she was all about, how old was I, and did I date boys, and my hair and clothes and all…she was snuggled up to me before we'd even sat down practically. I just…who would think? That I'd have sisters? And especially that I'd feel something for them the first time we ever met?"

Jay asked, "Lisa…do you know what Nicole told the girls? About you and how she gave you up…did she give the children details or not? What did they know about you?"

"I asked her the same questions ahead, because I wanted to be prepared. If I could be. Anyway, I guess she told them flat out that a long time ago she met a boy. She was too young to be too seriously involved, but no one could tell her anything at the time. She was still in high school when she found out she was pregnant." Lisa leaned back against her dad's knee. "She didn't tell the kids, but she told me—she wanted to get an abortion. But she didn't know she was pregnant for sure until after the third month. I don't quite get that…."

"She was pretty young, Lise," Ann said frankly. "There's every chance she wasn't regular. Or paying attention."

"I guess. But I don't see how she couldn't notice that she'd slept with a guy and then was missing periods. Even if she wasn't regular. Her sleeping with the guy would surely make her think."

Jay interrupted, "That's how *you* think, Lisa. That's how

we think. But a lot of people—not just young people—don't want to take responsibility for their actions. So they deny. Hope the problem'll disappear if they just pretend it doesn't exist."

"Well, personally I think that sucks," Lisa said.

Her dad offered her a thumbs-up. "Me, too."

"Anyway, the point is that Nicole apparently didn't realize she was pregnant until she was past three months. Then she couldn't make a decision about an abortion right away either, so more time passed, and by then…it was just pretty late in the day to do it. Or that's how she felt. And everybody, all the parents, the boyfriend, everyone, thought the same thing. That she was too young to be a mother. At least, a good mother. And when she went with her parents to the adoption agency—"

"They found us." Jay filled in the blank.

"Nicole said she knew the instant she met you two that you'd be fabulous parents. So then it all clicked in place for her, that adoption was the right thing to do." Lisa pushed at her hair. "I was hoping she'd tell me more about my birth father. And she said she would. Another time. I mean, I already know the health history and genetics and all that stuff, but…"

"You'd like to know more," Ann said gently. "Like why she fell in love with him. How he felt about the pregnancy."

"I knew you'd understand, Mom." Lisa hesitated.

"Nicole's been so great. But it's still kind of weird…she acts totally happy to meet me. To talk to me. But unless I'd shown up, I wonder if I'd even be a blip on her memory screen. I'm not trying to judge her for getting pregnant. At *all*. Or for giving me up. It's just that she makes it sound so easy. She just says she knew I was going to be in a fabulous home, so 'her heart was at rest.'"

Ann didn't, couldn't say anything, and neither did Jay. But Lisa finally spoke again.

"I'm just saying. My heart wouldn't have been at rest. To give up a baby. To know a baby of mine was alive in the world somewhere. To not know if it was sick or healthy, happy or hurting. I mean, how damn hard was it for her to use some birth control? Or, for that matter…it just seems weird to me that it was that easy for her to just go on, as if it never happened."

The phone rang…no surprise. With Lisa home, the phone was undoubtedly going to ring every six minutes. She bounced to her feet, but before charging off to answer the call, she said, "I'm just glad she's willing to see me again. That's all I'm saying. And for me to see my half sisters some more, too. Because otherwise, it'd just leave me with even more questions than I started with, you know?"

When the phone rang another couple times, she made a helpless gesture and then ran for it.

The TV screen was still frozen on the opening credits. Jay's hand was still on her back, but quietly, he shifted, returned to his chair and his *Journal*. "You were right, Ann," he said.

"About what?"

"I was worried when this came up. Her finding her birth mother, all that. I was afraid you'd get hurt. Afraid she would. But now…these are good questions she's raising. Not easy ones. But I think you were right to be quiet and just let her 'go' with this."

"Yes," Ann said. But her gaze seemed glued to the photographs in her hand. The two happy blond little girls looked so much like Lisa. Nicole was a beautiful woman, with the kind of tasteful, expensive, elegant look that Lisa could well have at that age. Her bone structure was classic.

Ann's own was…well, sturdy. Not heavy. She'd always watched her weight, been active. But she certainly didn't have ritzy-high cheekbones. Her hair could be a messy frizz fest on rainy days, nothing elegant about it. Even if her boobs weren't starting to sink, her hips starting to widen, she'd never had the capacity to look elegant and classic. She was Orvis, not Ellen Tracy. JC Penney, not Saks. It wasn't about money. Between her job and Jay's, they raked it in okay. It was just about taste and genetics.

She couldn't help her genes and was comfortable enough with her taste. But she was also aware that she tended to be invisible in a crowd.

That was fine with her. But Lisa…Lisa, like her birth

mother, had the look of a star. Gorgeous. Striking. A world apart from Ann's physical appearance.

Ann fingered the photos. Looks, of course, didn't matter. Love did. Their whole history with Lisa did. Looks just seemed like a symptom of a potential problem.

If there was a photograph of her and this Nicole standing next to Lisa, Ann knew perfectly well who'd look like the imposter.

Her.

Nicole, those children, looked so naturally like Lisa that it was as if they belonged together. Ann would look, the way she'd always felt, that she really belonged nowhere and to no one.

ON MONDAY AFTERNOON, Rose Marie took her customary defiant position on the window shelf, wearing high-heeled boots crossed at the ankles and a top showing more boobs than were legal. Or than should have been legal.

Ann had wheeled in a portable white board from two doors down—the one that was generally used for big powwows and major presentations. Using giant blue grease pens, she wrote a series of four letter words.

Rose Marie had made every effort to ignore her, but no matter how unwilling she was to participate, the obscene words clearly snared her attention. Finally she said, "What are you *doing?*"

"You recognize these words?"

"Of course I know those words!"

"I figured you might. Well, these words are all verbs." Ann cocked her head. "Actually, *verb* is another four letter word. Something I probably shouldn't be telling you about. The kind of word that can get you in big trouble if you say it in the wrong company, you know?"

"You're kidding." Rose Marie slid off her perch and ambled closer. "You're saying *verb* is another dirty word?"

"To some people," Ann said, thinking it was an honest answer. Sort of. And the end justified the means even if it wasn't kosher-honest.

"What's it mean?"

"Oh no. First, we're going to use these other words in sentences. Sentences that you're actually going to *read*, cookie. Not pretend. Really read. And then, we'll see...."

"If I do this crap, you'll tell me what the *verb* word means, though, right?"

Without a qualm, Ann promised, "If you do the work, I'll give you an unlimited number of four letter words to work with."

She left work that afternoon drained to beat the band, but pumping the air in triumph. She sped through traffic, anxious to get home to share the day with Lisa and Jay.

At a red light, she called a close friend of hers. "It worked," she crowed into her cell phone.

Nancy laughed. The two had found each other some five years before. Teaching reading wasn't supposed to be in Ann's job description, but the longer she worked with throwaway teens, the more she discovered they invariably had two things in common—lousy family backgrounds and illiteracy.

By accident, she'd come across Nancy—a special ed teacher. Counseling wasn't supposed to be in *her* job description, but she invariably found with her problem students that bad behavior often came with learning disabilities. She needed strategies. So did Ann. They'd regularly combined resources ever since, and the warmth of the developing friendship had surprised both of them.

"I can hear the glow in your voice—you're happy Lisa's home?"

Ann laughed. "Beyond belief."

"And Jay?"

"He's just as happy. He even watched *Charade* with us last night."

"Girl, that's love," Nancy said flatly.

"What can I say? I married a hero."

"Did I hear you mention Lisa was working over spring break?"

"Yeah. Just kind of lucked into it. Not a glamour job. Three kids, painting a neighbor's living and bedrooms. Great money for a week's work…although I know she'll come home tired tonight. I'm thinking of making something special, like a marinated tenderloin. And if I'm stuck turning on the oven, I might as well whip up a bread pudding and put that in, too, she loves it—"

"You spoil that girl."

"Darn right I do." Ann sighed. "I'm so lucky to have her to spoil." Traffic picked up; she rang off…but was still high enough to sing along with the radio at the top of her lungs. As she'd discovered long ago, other drivers did it, too.

Endorphins still pumping, she pulled in the drive, boogied into the house, and started fussing in the kitchen. Cooking wasn't the same without Lisa home. For just two of them— and Jay working crazy hours just like her—any kind of cooking seemed like a maintenance chore. With Lisa home, the fun of it was back. Making something new. Creating something fresh. Or remembering old favorites that they'd all forgotten about.

A half hour later, Jay ambled in. "I could smell dinner from the garage. That's it. We're never letting her go back to school again."

She laughed and lifted her face for his quick kiss and nuzzle on the neck. "We'll both gain five pounds while she's home."

"We'll survive it. Oh man. Dessert, too?"

She slapped his hand when he opened the oven door for a look. But then the phone rang. "You get it," she scolded, "I can't trust you in the kitchen alone."

"That's so unfair." But Jay plucked the landline…and then listened. She watched him suddenly turn around to her, look at her.

"What?" she mouthed.

"Lisa," he mouthed back, and then just said all right, okay, hon, that kind of thing, nothing that gave away information. When he hung up, he filled in the blanks.

"She won't be home for dinner, or a while. Nicole called her. The kids had some kind of game, and asked if Nicole would invite Lisa. She said she was tired, but didn't want to turn down a chance to get to know the girls better." He hesitated. "You okay with that?"

"Sure." She took a breath. "We both agreed we need to let her take this wherever she needs to, right? And as far as dinner…you're gonna love it."

Still Jay hesitated. So she slapped some hot pads in his hands and started handing out orders. "You're not getting a feast like this without doing some work," she teased.

And it worked. He quit looking at her that way, with that penetrating gaze, as if he feared she were going to break apart.

She wasn't a break-apart kind of cookie, never had been, felt insulted that he'd think she ever would be. And to reassure him that she was fine, totally fine, she buzzed around with the dinner, regaled him with the story about Rose Marie and the teaching-reading-via-swear-words strategy, then listened to his day…and Jay's day was always filled with patient stories. She used to tease him that he operated on the gut because that's what he always found in people. Their guts. Their gut heart, their gut values, their gut core.

The next morning, though, when Lisa came downstairs, Jay had already left for the hospital. Lisa was in fresh paint clothes and already in a rush, talking even as she wolfed down a blueberry muffin and handfuls of cereal. She tried to get into the bread pudding, but Ann yelped that it wasn't a breakfast food and there was plenty for later.

"Mom! I'm not a kid anymore! At school I'd have it, so why can't I have it here?"

"Because I'm still the mom," Ann said.

"How about a bite? One single small bite?"

So she had a bowlful, the whole time chattering about the night before. "Nicole drove us for ice cream afterwards, this place where they double churn it. I had English toffee."

And "Nicole wanted to know if I wanted a picture with me and the two girls. You know. She'd do a photography study with the three of us. Isn't that great?"

And "Nicole, it's so funny…she talks to me as if we were sisters, almost. I mean, you'd think we were never strangers. She called her mother about me, too, but I guess her mom had a car accident a few years ago…she's in a rest home. She's not that old. But she stroked out or something like that. Anyway, Nicole wasn't sure if it would register, but she still told her mother about me, told her she had another granddaughter…."

Okay, Ann kept saying to herself. It's all okay. But every word out of her daughter's mouth seemed to be "Nicole." And everything about Nicole seemed to fill in a whole extended family for Lisa…a family who could do no wrong, who delighted her at every turn. A family it was very easy, and very natural, for Lisa to love.

Nothing wrong about any of that.

Except that Ann felt more and more of an outsider in her daughter's life. And she didn't know what to do about that…except shut up and hold it in.

When Jay climbed under the covers in the dark bedroom, the window was cracked open. Mid April, the nights were still cold, but finally warm enough to let in some fresh air—and with it, the scent of hyacinths and daffodils. Ann wasn't a gardener any more than he was, but both of them had planted the wild, luxurious bed of bulbs years before. He wasn't admitting to being a hedonist—and neither would Ann. But the scent of spring flowers, especially on a dew-rich night, had to be close to the best smell in the universe.

The first best smell in the universe, though, was his wife's skin, fresh from a shower. She tiptoed into the bedroom, thinking he was already asleep. But she knocked over a paperback—the one she'd left on the dresser. Then something else, probably some cosmetic, when she fumbled for her hairbrush.

By the time she slid into bed next to him, her hair was freshly brushed—a ritual she did before sleeping every night—but her skin was still semi-damp. His wife had never completely dried herself after a shower. It was one of those idiosyncrasies that made her Ann. She thought she was dry; she never was. She thought she was quiet in the dark; she never was.

And she thought she was going straight to sleep, when Jay knew full well she was as tense as a spring.

She pulled up the comforter and immediately turned on her stomach. There was a time she'd never gone to sleep without whispering "I love you," but that tradition had been lost on the side of the road some time before.

He turned on his side, slowly, slowly, sliding a hand over shower-soft skin, starting with her smooth shoulder, palming the skin between her shoulder blades, moving to her spine. She neither moved nor objected. She simply went still, the way a rabbit went still when a wolf showed up.

He wasn't a wolf. Or Jay couldn't imagine thinking of himself as one. But that image often replayed in his mind, because a rabbit's defenses were similar to Ann's. She tried to be invisible when she wanted a problem to disappear. She froze rather than running. And Jay strongly suspected she had no idea how tightly she was holding herself…how much she was holding back. Not just from him. But from herself.

He did.

He did the itsy bitsy spider routine with his fingers, walking up her vertebrae, up to the knots at the nape of her neck, into her scalp…and then he had her. Ann wasn't just a hopeless sucker for a head rub. She'd sell her mother and soul for one. A groan sieved out of her throat like a woman in enormous pain. Or pleasure.

It was a good start.

She'd been so hurt. He still didn't totally grasp why this had hit her so hard. Obviously he understood the problem was something about Lisa and Lisa's birth mom. Ann kept saying it was all right. That Lisa needed to know the answers about her birth mother and father that she was seeking. That the relationship with Nicole threatened nothing of what she and Jay had brought to Lisa.

In other words, she kept saying all the right things. The intelligent things. The rational things.

Only in the weeks since the word *Nicole* had become a regular part of Lisa's vocabulary, he'd watched Ann become more tense, more quiet. Her natural effusiveness dimmed. Her smiles were more rote. And God knew, she fought him getting close.

His hands kneaded, rubbed, caressed. Seduced. Jay thought it darkly ironic, that he still had to seduce his wife of twenty years. God knew, she'd taken all his skill and con-artist techniques back when they were teenagers—and it had taken every wily way he had, first to get her shirt off, then her bra, and those silky underpants of hers was one long-term challenge. She'd never parted with anything willingly.

But when she gave in…she gave in completely. Not 100 percent, but 500 percent. Not with just her body, but surrendering her heart and soul as well…as she did now. The darkness folded around them like a secret blanket when she suddenly turned, wrapping her arms and legs around him, tugging him down.

She wanted deep, hard strokes this night. She wanted passion, not tenderness. She wanted a wild, rough ride, not the slow hands routine. She wanted sweat and hot oblivion.

He did his damnedest to give her what she wanted.

Later, when she was sprawled on his chest, sleeping so deep he doubted a cannon would wake her, he kept stroking her back. He was still wide awake. Replete for the moment, yet feeling less and less sure where his place was in her life. Husband, yes. But that was just a word. In itself it didn't convey whether he mattered to her, whether he was important to her, if their marriage was something she took for granted on a par with needing shoes in the winter…on a par with something she wanted, the way they'd once wanted each other, as wonderfully and desperately as air and water.

Elementally.

You couldn't be nineteen again? That stupid and foolish, that wildly, recklessly in love?

But where Ann seemed to feel that she had lost her place in Lisa's life…he felt increasingly lost in hers.

SATURDAY MORNING, Ann lugged two grocery sacks in the door, and barely managed to kick the door closed before a sneeze bigger than Alaska shook her body from the inside out.

Jay showed up in the kitchen doorway, shook his head and then hiked forward to take the groceries. "You're soaked to the bone."

"That's probably because it's raining, you think?"

"It's called pouring. And you've already got a cold. Did I tell you I'd do the shopping this week or what?"

"You told me. But the last time you went grocery shopping, we had five bags of Doritos and no lettuce or toilet paper."

"So maybe we could have survived that week without lettuce. Or vegetables for that matter."

"What is it, something in the Y chromosome that blocks out any information about nutrition? And you're a doctor besides." They sniped back and forth until the groceries were in, put away and a long, tall glass of microwaved tea put in front of her. She added cold medicine. Times two.

Ann freely admitted she was suffering a major case of cold depression. How could anything look good when your head felt the size of a balloon? She couldn't shake the crabbiness. Outside, the pouring rain was turning everything spring green, but nothing could tempt her into seeing anything fresh or inviting.

Lisa had been back to school a couple of weeks now. The house was always quiet. Hollow, she thought. No more noise or messes. No reason to make sinful foods with a ton of cholesterol. No reason to feel that burst of a rush to get home from work.

She liked her work, her life, her house. Just not today.

"Drink," Jay ordered her. "I'll make some soup for lunch." He added quickly, "As soon as I find it."

He was so hopeless in the kitchen that Ann just put her chin in her hand and watched the comedy play out. That man had a reputation across the country for what he could do with a scalpel, but opening a simple can of soup and heating it darn near burned up his brain cells for the day.

She feared he might be permanently brain damaged when she suddenly heard him say, "I know you're miserable now. But what do you think about taking off two weekends from Friday? Fly to New York. Or Boston. Whichever."

"I don't understand. What do you mean, take off?"

"You know. Take off. Steal a weekend to ourselves. Do some nice restaurants, stay in a nice place. Hear some music at night, and during the day, just pick something you want to do—a play, if you want. Or even shop."

She stared at him dumbfounded. Jay offering to shop was as likely as the moon turning pink. "You're ill," she said. "I knew you couldn't maintain the impossible schedule you've been on. It's no surprise that the long hours finally caught up with you. I told you you were working too hard—"

"Hey. It's not like we never stole away for a weekend before."

"Not in years. We don't do that kind of thing anymore."

"Yup. That's the point," Jay said genially, although when he took his first spoonful of soup, he grimaced. "Why didn't you tell me it was cold? Anyway. Pick your city and we'll do it up."

He tried to take her bowl, but she was almost finished, so there was no point in heating it now. Besides, she was too confounded by the conversation to think of anything else. She and Jay hadn't gone off alone together since she could remember—for all the obvious reasons.

"Neither of us have any time," she reminded him.

"Exactly why we need to make some. I doubt either of us could arrange a whole week right now. But surely we could shake free for a three-day weekend."

"Plane tickets will cost a fortune, making arrangements this quickly."

"Yeah," Jay agreed. "Which is another reason we haven't done this before. Because when we try to plan too far ahead, something always happens, with either your work or mine or Lisa. And then we both say tickets will cost too much if we have to buy them on the spur of the moment. Which they probably will. So what? We can afford it."

"We don't know what Lisa's plans are—"

"Fine. So ask her. If she was planning on coming home that weekend, then we'll go the one after that."

"Boston," she murmured, her tongue rolling around the

sound of it. "New York," she murmured, seeing if her tongue liked the sound of that one better. "Both sound...."

"Sound what?"

She glanced at Jay. Even through rheumy eyes and a head thick with cold, she noticed he suddenly looked oddly tense, oddly still. "Both sound totally wonderful," she said.

And there went the starch in his shoulders. "Maybe we can do both then. New York now. Boston in a few months."

"Something's gotten into you," she said severely. "I don't know what it is, but I want my husband back. I can't go around sleeping with a stranger." She wanted to whack herself upside the head. His lunacy must be catching, because she seemed to be flirting. With her own husband.

Which might be fun—or at least an interesting option— if he wasn't looking at a woman with a red nose and no makeup. Her jeans were baggy and her hair hadn't been washed in two nights. She looked nothing like the girl he'd fallen in love with. In fact, she figured she looked worse than the witch in Macbeth.

"Who knows," Jay said. "I might just turn into a stranger in New York. And you might like sleeping with an unknown guy for a weekend."

Her eyes narrowed. "Well, you're not sleeping with an unknown woman. Ever, buster. So don't even try fantasizing down that road."

For some insane reason, he looked delighted with her. In

fact, as he retrieved his soup bowl to heat up in the micro-wave, he started whistling. Even when he overheated the soup and it bubbled over. Even when he had to clean that up and then the soup was still too hot to eat.

Whistling, Ann thought. The man was addled. And more addling yet was discovering that she felt more rotten than rot…yet she was suddenly tempted to start whistling, too.

He sent her off to bed after lunch. Actually, she didn't go to bed, but curled up in the den under an old down comforter, with the remote locked on LMN and a box of Kleenex stashed next to her.

He brought a fresh mug of tea for her. She told him then she wouldn't sleep because she couldn't breathe. He said, "uh-huh" in that tone of voice that justified husband-homicide in a lot of wives' minds.

The next thing she knew, the phone was ringing. She grabbed it, coming awake at the same time, only to realize that the world had changed. The lamps were lit. The TV on Nascar. And Jay had obviously been sitting there for some time, because he was in stocking feet with a book in his hand and the absconded remote.

"Hey, Mom, it's Lisa."

"Hey, baby." Ann glanced at her watch, then the Herman Miller clock on the bookcase. Both claimed it was past five in the afternoon, which obviously was impossible. She'd laid down right after lunch.

"I've got an idea."

Ann heard the peppy, perky tone in her daughter's voice and tried to prop her eyes open. The nap had helped, but damn, the cold was still there, still making her head feel thicker than mud. "What?" she asked, hoping her voice projected some enthusiasm.

"I was talking to Nicole...and then I started thinking...wouldn't it be a great idea if we all went to dinner together? Then she could meet you and Dad. I know she'd like to. And you could meet her and my two half sisters. We could all get to know one another, you know? Wouldn't that be great?!"

Ann pushed herself to a sitting position, feeling her stomach suddenly thud. "Well...did you have a time in mind for this?"

"Yeah. I talked to Nicole. So I was thinking, like two weeks from Saturday. If you and Dad are free then?"

Ann tried to think of an excuse to beg off, but nothing popped into her mind. The sick feeling in her stomach was hardly a reason she could explain to her daughter. And Lisa knew perfectly well that she and Jay generally reserved Saturday nights for a dinner out, so it would be unlikely they suddenly had other plans.

A tickle built in her nose. She reached for a Kleenex just as a sneeze the size of Vesuvius erupted. Lucky it didn't shake the house. Unfortunately it didn't clear any brain cells...in her heart, she just plain didn't want to meet

Nicole. Didn't want to meet Nicole's family. Didn't want their two families to get together.

But in her head, she realized that was ridiculous. It was some kind of stupid jealousy or insecurity that not only shamed her, but made her want to hide those feelings so Lisa would never know.

Besides which, that reaction was so darn *dumb*. She and Jay had raised Lisa. She had no reason—none—to believe anyone could threaten the outstanding mom-daughter relationship they had.

But there it was. The irrational fear that Lisa would love Nicole more than her.

"Mom? You okay? Sounds like you've got a heckuva head cold."

"I do, I do." She struggled to pull herself together, to chase away those ugly feelings once and for all—and before Lisa realized she had them. "Honey, if you want to do this…maybe I could have them for dinner here. Just to have a more comfortable atmosphere than a restaurant, you know? And if you'd like Nicole to meet us, then they could see how we live as well. And the girls could have the TV, computers, something to do if they get bored with a bunch of adult talk."

"Oh, that'd be even better! It'd be so much easier to just hang out and talk at home. That's *great*, Mom!"

When Ann clicked off the phone, she sank back against

the couch pillows...and only then realized that Jay had muted the TV and was staring hard at her.

"What in *hell* are you doing, Ann?" He said it so low, so quiet, that she felt the oddest stab of anxiety.

"What do you mean?" She said "hell." He said "hell." Both of them said a ton of words in various circumstances, but she couldn't remember his using hell when talking about her, talking to her. Not that way. It...startled her.

It wasn't as if she and Jay never argued. They could both work up a good huff over politics, bicker over money, fight over all the usual stuff—but, in general, they both hated confrontations. They both seemed to crave peace, maybe partly because their outside lives were so busy and stressful. They both tried to bring peace to each other. Or so she'd always thought.

Jay stood up. And now she could see his neck was flushed, his eyes snapping with emotion. "I mean what I said. What the *hell* were you thinking?"

She started to answer, but then a series of sneezes took her over. She grabbed for the Kleenex and discovered the box was empty.

Jay muttered another "hell," stomped off, came back with the box of tissues from the bathroom and then said, "Obviously you feel rotten. I realize that. This is no time to talk about anything. Forget it for now."

"No, I don't want to forget it—" But he was already gone,

stalked out of the room. Sick or not sick, cold or no cold, she really didn't want to leave the conversation hanging that way. Not when Jay was so obviously upset. Really upset.

But when she lurched off the couch and tried to chase after him, it seemed he'd grabbed a jacket and headed outside. Both cars sat in the garage, and both keys hung in their usual spot by the door, so he didn't intend to drive anywhere. But the rug by the back door had skidded sideways, and he'd left the back porch light on, both clues that he'd taken off in a hurry and didn't necessarily intend to be back for a while.

Jay was a walker. So was she. But he'd pretty obviously left to work off his anger and Ann felt a spear of anxiety. It was one thing to have a fight about money or politics or who left the car without gas…and another to not have a clue why Jay was upset—much less why he was upset with her.

She resolved to corner him the minute he came back in…but it was late, and she was conked out with more cold medicine by then.

The next morning, he got a call ultra early, and had left the house for the hospital before she was out of bed. And then she ended up calling in sick, because it seemed crazy to work with kids when she was sneezing and coughing to beat the band. They'd just catch whatever she had. So for the rest of that day, she socked in, did the liquids and vitamin-C and snuggle-up thing, only roused long enough to put something in the oven for dinner…except that she couldn't connect with Jay that night either, because he didn't make it home until past ten.

His schedule was always unpredictable, and hers wasn't perfect either, so there wasn't anything unusual about their not being able to connect for a day or two at a time. Still, this was different because she hated an unsettled problem between them.

She especially hated Jay being mad at her, because, darn it, he almost never was. Their spats were usually about stuff, not each other. She couldn't remember a single time they'd lasted longer than a short huff. This steady, quiet chill coming off Jay didn't scare her exactly…but it definitely rattled her.

They finally caught up on Thursday, as it happened, in the garage. When she pulled in from work, Jay was standing, hands on hips, glaring at the lawn mower.

He glanced at her when he heard the car, then went back to that furious stare at the lawn mower. She knew the ritual, knew enough to slowly, cautiously approach. She stood next to him for several moments, hands on hips, too, until she got around to heaving an empathetic sigh. "Well? Are we going to get rid of the damned thing or squeak another year out of it?"

He said, "It didn't start. It won't start. So I can take it back to the repair shop, and we can get it fixed, and claim the warrantee thing and bring it back home. And that would be just hunky dory, except that as soon as we bring it back home—you know as well as I do—it won't work. Either it won't start or it won't cut or something else will be wrong."

Midway through April, they'd mowed the grass once. Now, as they both knew, it was almost tall enough to bail. Armies of puppies and children could hide in the lawn, it was that high. Lost earrings or quarters didn't have a chance.

Their neighbors, who all manicured their lawns within an inch of their lives, hadn't given them any tsk-tsk looks yet, but if they didn't start keeping up the neighborhood landscaping standards, they would.

Standing hip-bumping close, Ann felt kin to her one ally in the battle of the lawns. "This lawn mower," she said, "has hated us from the day we brought it home."

"It's a machine, Ann. It doesn't have emotions."

"This one does. No matter how well we treat it, it doesn't care. It's a sociopath."

Jay looked like he wanted to give her another Y chromosome type of comment, but then seemed to discover his better sense. "I know. But it just seems crazy to throw out a lawn mower that isn't even two years old."

"It's a lemon. It was born a lemon and it's going to die a lemon. Is it worth our both getting ulcers over it?"

They stared at it some more. Then Jay said, "It's not the money I mind. But if we were going to throw money away, we could go on a vacation for this kind of bucks. Or put in a hot tub outside. Or get the new couch you keep saying we need but nobody can seem to find time to shop for. Buying a new lawn mower just feels like throwing money down a black pit."

"Because it is. It completely sucks," Ann agreed. And while they were getting along so well, she slipped in, "For God's sake, Jay, why were you so mad at me?"

"I'm not mad at you."

"You were. Sunday night."

He frowned, then finally turned away from the offending and offensive machine. "Are we going to throw out this sucker and buy a new one?"

"Yup."

"Then let's hit Lowe's and then get some dinner."

Jay never shopped if he could conceivably help it. When they needed something, either he left it up to her to pick out and buy, or—with something as major as a lawn mower—he'd go. But he'd pick out the best quality product he could identify, buy it lickety-split, and then escape the store as if he were hustling to get out of Dodge.

So less than an hour later, they were already at dinner. They'd mutually picked the corner booth of Ma Baker's, an old-fashioned bar with the hottest chili this side of Mexico. "This'll clear your sinuses for once and all," he said.

"Is that your best medical advice, Doc?"

It seemed the first time in days he'd been relaxed. The

bar had an easy, natural atmosphere, half the walls done up in green and white—for Michigan State, the other half in blue and gold, for the University of Michigan. It was more a neighborhood haunt than a drinking hole. People came to get their throats burned out on the chili or to catch up with friends. And Ann figured she'd have to crowbar the problem from last weekend out of Jay, but once they settled into dinner, he came right out with it.

"You agreed to a dinner with Nicole and her two girls?"

"Yes." But Ann blinked. That was the big hairy problem?

"And you told Lisa that you wouldn't mind having the dinner at our house?"

"Yes," Ann affirmed for a second time, even more curious where this was headed.

"Call it off, Ann."

His voice had turned quiet—that upsetting quiet the way it had before—but Ann was still confounded as to why. "Huh? Come on. You've got to spill out better than this what's on your mind."

Jay started to do just that and then stopped, as if the issue had become so huge that he couldn't get it all out in one lump. He took a pull on his long neck, looked around the bar at the other couples huddled over their dinners, and then finally back at her. His dark eyes were fiercely intense. His jaw, set sharp as a bone.

"What Lisa is doing with Nicole…finding her birth

mother, figuring out where her birth mother fits in with her identity and all that stuff…it's all fine. Just fine. But that part is about Lisa. It's not about you and me. It doesn't need to come into our home."

She stopped eating. "Honestly, I don't have a clue what you mean. Are you saying you don't want Nicole and the girls in our house?"

"No. I'm saying *you* don't."

Her eyes narrowed. Jay should have known better than to wave a red flag in front of a bull. "You're telling me what I feel?"

Now he quit eating, too. Folded his arms. "No bullshit now."

"I wasn't giving you any." But somehow she was managing to build up a case of fury by then. It was either that or worry why Jay seemed almost a stranger. And why he was angry when she hadn't done a darn thing to earn it.

But he seemed to think she had. "You're going crazy over this Nicole business," he told her. "Lisa doesn't realize how much it's upsetting you. And there's no reason it has to, for God's sake. Just back off."

"What makes you think I'm going crazy?"

"Hell. We've been married how long? I understand why you're hiding it from Lisa. You don't want her to think you're touchy about developing a relationship with Nicole. But this is *me*. I *know* what a mountain this is for you. I can see it. And I've had it with just shutting up and watching you get more and more tight about this. Having a dinner for them—it's just ridiculous."

"I don't know where you got all this, but it's totally not true." When Jay said nothing, she immediately repeated, "I am *fine* with Lisa getting to know Nicole."

"Yeah. Like you'd be fine with a case of pneumonia."

"Jay. I didn't say I totally *liked* it. But I have no doubt at all that our relationship with Lisa is as stable as Mount Everest. I can't imagine anything breaking that bond. There's no reason in the universe why her getting to know her birth mother should threaten us. It doesn't take away from anything we have for her. She knows we love her. We know she loves us."

"You can sell that story to somebody else, because it isn't working with me. You're totally right, Ann. You shouldn't feel threatened, even remotely. But you do. And that's the point. I'd like to think you could tell me how you feel."

"I talk to you all the time!"

"If you could talk to me—really talk to me—you could have gotten it off your chest from the start. About how much this has been tearing you up."

"It's *not* tearing me up."

Jay threw up his hands and then stood. "I give up. You're not eating and I'm not eating. So there's no point wasting any more time on this."

She completely agreed. But whether he was talking about

dinner or their fight, she wasn't sure. Either way, they both stormed from the restaurant, driving home with a heavy, pregnant silence on both their sides.

By the time he brought the paper into the den, though, he asked her evenly if there was a decent movie on.

She responded evenly that there was a choice of two they both might like.

So they were speaking again. Just not about Lisa. Or about each other. Ann told herself there was nothing really wrong. They'd bickered before, and just the way other married people developed patterns, they had theirs. First they did that huffy puffy thing for a while, then carefully did the ultra-polite thing for a while and eventually they went back to normal.

She was sure it would be like that this time, too.

Or almost sure.

There seemed to be a spear in her heart that had never been there before.

She and Jay had been solid for so long that she couldn't remember fearing anything wrong with their marriage. Now...well, there was a rip. And beneath that rip, surprising her, scaring her, was a vulnerability that made her feel shakily unsure. Of herself. Of Jay. Of *them*.

The worst part of Ann's job, she felt, was having to pass on the kids to the next step. Once she'd been made advisor to the juvenile court, she'd fought the system to get the kids longer than just through the old-time evaluation process. By giving her specific work time with the kids, she'd proven that she could give a more accurate evaluation—and that had proven to give the kids a better shot at survival back in the real world.

But still. Ann felt as if she were abandoning a child when it was move-on time. Especially when the child had been thrown away as often as Rose Marie had been.

Friday afternoon, the sky was a blustery gray, the two of them holed up in Ann's office for the last time. "You'll get passed onto a real reading teacher from here, instead of just a faker. But you've also got some decisions in front of you. You'll be doing community service for months, but you have choices about what those will be. You could clean up trash from the roads." Ann weighed an imaginary scale in her hands. "Or you could work at a senior citizens' facility doing chores—fetch-and-carrying, changing lightbulbs, that kind of thing."

"In other words, a lot of work," Rose Marie said disparagingly.

"Sure is. Plus, you won't get paid for doing community service. *But*…if you build up a reputation at the facility, my guess is that you could build up steady work. Good money, because there are lots of people over 65 who just need a little help. If you get listed on a seniors group or two for being reliable, you could actually turn this into something. Of course, you could also completely screw it up."

Rose rolled her eyes with a weary sigh. "I am so *not* going to miss you."

"Yeah, I'm not going to miss you either, Ms. Attitude."

"I've still got a long way to go on the reading. I don't see why I have to work with someone else."

"I do. I just got reading on the table for you, but now you need a real live reading teacher to take you where you want to go. And I hear the doubt in your voice, but don't make light of the breakthroughs you've accomplished. You're on your way. I see tons of kids, cookie, where I just know I'm going to see them right back in the system in a matter of months. They don't want to change. They don't want to admit they could be at fault for anything. They're angry and they want to stay angry. They don't really want to fix anything."

"Yeah, well, maybe that's me, too."

"No, it's not. You've got a real shot, Rose. You can do it.

Turn your life around. I know you had a rough start, but I believe in you. Believe you're really on your way."

An hour later, Ann left the courthouse, feeling clicking-heels upbeat. Her job never had clean-cut happy endings, only possibilities, but some days—corny or not—she just plain loved it. As she strode toward the covered parking lot, she turned her cell phone on—she never took calls at work if she could help it—and immediately saw a message from Lisa.

Before climbing in her car, she managed to reach her. The view from the open lot was stupendous. Typical of the last week in April, spring flowers and blossoms spilled in every direction, filling the senses with those scents and colors. The lawns looked like green velvet, the flowering crab and pear beyond lush. She could barely think for all the winsome, woosome smells out there. When it came down to it, the whole spring smelled like falling in love….

"Hey, Mom. I just wanted to know if you wanted me to come early to help with the dinner tomorrow."

"It's just an extra three, no big sweat to pull off. Actually, I'm sorry Nicole's husband couldn't come to round it all out. Anyway, the earlier you get here, the better, but not to work, just so we'll have more time to talk."

"I can make it right after lunch, I think. Is that okay?"

"Sure."

"What are you going to have for dinner, Mom?"

"Oh…I'm going to leave that for a surprise."

Well, that was almost the truth, Ann considered on the way home. Dinner was definitely going to be a surprise, because she had no clue yet what to have. Her first problem was being no great cook. Then, she didn't want the dinner to be too formal, because that would stiffen everybody up, and make it look as if she'd gone to piles of trouble. The menu had to be something two little girls would be willing to eat. And it had to be something fool-proof—because she'd been known to burn or goof up anything too fancy.

Besides needing to grocery shop for the food, she was going home tonight to do a major house clean. Only she'd barely gotten home to start that before she ran into glitches that required a serious shopping run.

She hadn't noticed before, but the downstairs bathroom needed new guest towels. And the kitchen towels suddenly looked pitiful, too. And since she had to go for those things, she bought new bath rugs, the big fluffy kind, because she'd been planning to replace those around summer, anyway. Raspberry, this time.

Then she figured that with six, they were going to have to eat in the dining room, so she might as well pop for new, fresh place mats and napkins. Real napkins. But in a color-ful, fun stripe that didn't look too formal.

Past nine o'clock, she got around to the food shopping,

deciding on dessert first. Kids didn't seem particularly fond of pie today, so she opted for an Apple Kuchen recipe that had been passed down in the family—one of Lisa's favorites. And then chicken Parmesan, which was one of the chicken recipes even she couldn't screw up, and another of Lisa's favorites, and kids always seemed to like it. Then she tried to think of side dishes. And some snacks ahead, like smoked Brie on crackers, but she had to find something less fuddy-duddy for the kids....

"Darn it, don't you say a word," she told Jay, when she found him standing in the doorway on Saturday morning with his hands on his hips.

"Did I speak?" Jay asked, with the wounded tone of a hurt dog.

"No. But you were thinking it. There's nothing wrong. Everything's great. This has been a lot of fun to prepare for. I'm looking forward to it. We're going to have a great time. We—"

"Okay, okay." Jay lifted his hands in the universal gesture of surrender. "I was just going to ask if I could use the towels in the downstairs bathroom."

"*No.* Or the soap!"

"Got it. Do I have any instructions for this extremely casual, no-fuss dinner tonight?"

"Yeah. Would you take on the drinks, whatever anyone wants, if you could handle that—"

"Got it. And while we're on the subject of orders, do you have any instructions on what I'm supposed to wear."

"Of course not. You can wear anything you want." Ann said frowning. "Except nothing too expensive, because Nicole doesn't sound that well off. We don't want to look like we're showing off. And nothing too formal, because we want everybody to relax…but nothing so casual it'd look like we didn't care about their coming—"

"Um, Ann? This is an offer you're not gonna get everyday, so if I were you I'd go with it. Just tell me what to wear. Period. No explanation."

"Oh. Oh, well…like a long-sleeved polo. Your blue one. And just some chinos."

"Any other orders?"

She charged over to him, dishtowel in one hand, a spoon in the other, and bussed him on the cheek. "You're being damned nice," she said.

"I'm always nice."

"Uh-huh." But he didn't have to be about this, especially since the scrapes from their fight on this still hadn't healed. He'd shut up completely as he'd watched her go into the preparation frenzy. And now, he was being cute about going along instead of obstructive.

She suspected it was causing him an ulcer not to comment or argue further. It was causing her an ulcer not to have a further chance to defend herself. And another ulcer to present an infernally-ever-cheerful smile on her face for the last several days, no matter what went wrong, or how whipped she was from putting this all together.

When Lisa popped in the door just after one, though, Ann was ready for Armageddon, and had the practiced, relaxed smile to prove it.

"I can smell the Apple Kuchen!" Lisa shrieked, as she zoomed toward the kitchen, leaving a wake of shoes, purse, jacket and dirty laundry.

Ann trailed after her like a hound. "Don't touch until dinner."

"Mom! You made chicken Parmesan! I love you!"

"I love you, too, baby."

"And oh-my-God, you're gonna make cheddar mashed potatoes?"

Chaos ensued—the same chaos that always ensued when Lisa got in the door. She said she wanted to take a fast shower—which she did, only she opted to use the bathroom downstairs, taking out the fresh towels and new soap. And then she came out, wearing holey jeans and flip-flops and a shirt from high school.

"Mom, this isn't a dress-up dinner. It's just Nicole. And I told them you weren't fussing."

"And I'm not," Ann assured her. "I was just chuckling at how old that shirt of yours is."

"Yeah," Lisa said blissfully. "Coming home always makes me feel like wearing comfort clothes. Where's Dad?"

"Last I knew, your dad was in the backyard—" Only the phone chose just that moment to ring. The hospital. And though Ann knew perfectly well Jay wasn't happy about this dinner, she'd still counted on him being next to her. Instead a patient was apparently having some kind of post-surgery crisis, and he had to go.

She'd been a doctor's wife too long not to expect interruptions like that. It was just *today*.

"I shouldn't be long," Jay said.

"Whatever it takes. You know what I'm making. Everything will taste just as good warmed up, so don't worry about it."

"Ann." Even though he'd pulled on his jacket and was clearly ready to leave, he came back toward her and curled his hands around her shoulders. "Don't get yourself in a tizzy over this."

"Hey. Have I ever been a tizzy kind of woman before?"

"No," he said. "Not before." And then looked hard in her eyes before smooching her forehead. "Only about this. But you're definitely tizzy about this. Just try to keep it together."

She was so insulted, she almost got blistery. She'd never needed taking care of, wasn't a needy kind of woman and hugely resented Jay implying she was. Still, she let him get away with it, because she didn't want Lisa to realize how stressed she was—and even besides that, doctors' wives had an unspoken code not to start an argument before your husband was going into a life or death situation. It just wasn't fair.

So she'd just have to chew him out later. Like the very instant they had two seconds alone.

For now, she was not only busy preparing for dinner, but she had Lisa all to herself until the group got there. Although both of them ran nonstop between the kitchen and dining room, conversation still spread like butter on hot toast, smooth and nonstop and delicious.

The old boyfriend was out. Someone named Mike was in the picture now—but definitely not serious. Too cute. Guys who were too cute were always trouble. She was looking at summer jobs, already offered two in Ann Arbor, but she really wanted to be home for the summer, what did Ann think? Haircuts. Spring colors. Scandals on campus. Family news. Ann's job. Lisa's roommate's pregnancy scare. An old classmate volunteering for Iraq. Two kids at school who knew Dad; Jay had operated on someone in their families. Should Lisa add highlights for the summer? Should Ann?

It was just chat. Just fussing with each other.

Ann kept thinking, why on *earth* had she ever believed she could lose her daughter? Or that anyone could get between them?

And how could she have been so *small* as to be jealous of Lisa needing to know about her birth mother? All the nerves she'd been going through—and trying to hide—disappeared completely over the next couple hours of chatter and laughter and messing around.

By the time the doorbell rang at four, Ann not only beat Lisa to the door, but had an enthusiastically welcoming smile as she greeted the three blondes. "Come on in, I'm so so glad to meet you all!"

And she was.

For the first ten minutes.

Nicole, Emily and Samantha—alias Sammie—were all dressed alike…identical to Lisa, for that matter. Everybody was wearing snug jeans over long, skinny legs, and big oversized tops, precisely the kind of ultra-casual attire that Lisa had probably encouraged them to dress in. It was just that Ann had chinos and a V-neck navy sweater, thinking that'd be safe. Only it wasn't safe. Next to everyone else, she felt a thousand times more dated and old.

Still, vanity had nothing to do with hostessing issues, and she hustled to make everyone comfortable. Sammie, the eleven-year-old athletic one, clomped in and zoned on the tube. She was the easiest to please. Give her a soda and cookies and a remote, and she was happy.

Emily, whose little jeans were decorated with pink ponies down the side, whose blond hair was a web of curls and clips, clung tight to her mother until Ann unearthed some old games of Lisa's. Then Lisa took her over, sitting on the floor, while the two set up characters and cards for a Clue game. Sammie eventually joined in.

For a while, there was just Ann and Nicole in the kitchen. "Would you like wine? Or a soda? Jay was hoping to be here—and he still will be—but he got called to the hospital. I'm hoping it won't be long."

Nicole looked tall and svelte and *young*. "Your house is so fabulous. And I hope we get to meet Jay, too. The house…you…just everything…you're just what I dreamed for my daughter."

The *"my"* daughter bit like a wasp. Ann was so stung she didn't know what to say, but that was all right, because Nicole went on. And on.

"It's just so awesome, that she found me after all these years. That I could get to know her—and now to get a chance to see how she was raised, how she's lived. I've done all right since marrying this last time, but it was a struggle when the girls were younger. And I still can't compete with the kind of wealth and advantages you've given our Lisa."

Again, the *"our"* grated like salt on a bee sting. But again, Nicole kept talking so Ann didn't have to.

"I have to admit, I felt awkward at first. It was tough to tell Sammie and Emily that I'd made a mistake, when they're of an age asking questions about boys and sex. And I'm trying to teach them the right values. But I started thinking…maybe that's why Lisa came back into our lives at this point. So I could admit to a mistake. And admit to doing the right thing about it, standing up, giving up my child even though I totally, totally loved and wanted her, but doing the thing that mattered—giving her the best life possible…."

The damn woman was beautiful, which wouldn't particularly bother Ann, except that Nicole and the girls all looked like Lisa. They were all so blond. So classic-boned. So lean and elegant shaped.

So not like her.

Ann kept watching the clock, thinking she could hold dinner for a bit, but as one hour passed and then the next, the children had to be hungry and Jay still wasn't home. So she served. Lisa inhaled the feast, laughing as the girls gobbled it down with her same enthusiasm.

"My favorites," she told them. "Don't you think it's a clue how related we are? That you all love chicken Parmesan as much as I do? And wait until you taste dessert."

When the girls laughed, they sounded like a younger Lisa. And the way Lisa held her fork, Ann could see, was just how Nicole did. Not a copycat thing or anything like that—more as if there were some genetic propensity to hold a fork a certain way, to cock one's head just so when listening to a certain conversation, to giggle with a certain alto pitch. All four of them had a natural part on the right side of their heads. All four of them crossed their legs the same way.

"Ann, this is just marvelous. You're such a great cook!"

"Thanks," Ann said. "Ready for dessert, everyone?"

They were. Still, Jay wasn't home, but Ann scooped up big squares of Kuchen for the crew—who fell on the dessert as if they hadn't leveled huge platters at dinner. All she heard was wow, how great, and man is this good, and you went to so much trouble, Ann…but when the subject reverted back to real conversation, the girls talked solely to each other. The topics were music and school, hated classes and school rituals. The two youngsters clearly adored Lisa, revered her as an older sister…which, of course, she was….but their hero-worship saddened Ann, because God knew, she'd have had a dozen kids if she could have. She'd always fiercely wanted to fill up a house with kids to bicker together and hero-worship each other and just be a *family*.

A family like the four blondes at the table just naturally seemed to be.

"All right now." Nicole stood up. "Ann, you went to all the trouble of preparing all this, so I'm doing the dishes for you and no arguing."

"That's not necessary—"

"Of course it is. It just isn't fair otherwise. Besides, Lisa'll help me and show me where everything goes, right, Lise?"

"Sure."

So Nicole and Lisa took over her kitchen and Ann was banished to the living room. By then, the littlest one—Emily—had warmed up, and being the cuddle-bug she was, snuggled next to Ann while Sammie dealt the cards. Crazy Eights was the game.

Once, Emily sneaked a look at her hand and said gently, "Honestly, you don't have to cheat so we'll win. We win plenty. Besides, we like you."

And another time, Emily said, "You know, I'm getting really confused."

"About what, honey?" Ann asked.

"Mom had sex before she was supposed to. I got all that. That's how a girl gets pregnant, I know all that, too. Only the thing is, is Lisa really Mom's or yours? I mean, can she be both of yours? And does that mean, I could have another mommy, too?"

Oh, God. It was the kind of question Ann loved. Sticky. Complicated. Riddled with emotional landmines. The kind of question that would have given her a maternal orgasm— if Lisa had asked it. But little Emily wasn't her child, and anything she said, no matter how careful or honest, could conflict with however Nicole wanted to treat such issues.

So she said, "You have one mommy. Your mommy. Eventually, when you get older, you may get married, and then your husband will probably have a mom, too. And that person won't be *your* mom exactly, but she'll be what's called a mother-in-law. So there are actually lots of ways to get other moms."

Emily considered this. "Kind of like when you call people 'aunt' when they're not really your aunt?"

"Very much like that. A real aunt is a real aunt and a real mom is a real mom. Nobody takes the place of your *real* mom. But still, there are a bunch of ways in life that we get to add some people who matter to us. They may not be our moms, but they can be kind of *like* moms."

"She's pretty dumb," Sammie pointed out, with a nod toward her younger sister. "She's always got questions like that."

Emily's eyes welled. "I'm not dumb. And I have another question. If Lisa gets my mom for another mom, then do Sammie and I get you for our extra mom?"

The eleven-year-old heaved another heavy sigh. "She can go on for hours with the questions, I'm warning you. No matter how much you answer, she'll just ask more and more."

"I'm not dumb," Emily repeated and then socked her sister.

That was when Nicole and Lisa strode in, to what was apparently a familiar tease-and-howl game between sisters...but one Ann hadn't managed to control very well. Through the din—and Nicole looking at her as if shocked she'd done something to upset the youngsters—Ann in honed on her daughter's face.

"The dishes are done, Mom," Lisa said. But the look of vibrance and animation she'd had through the whole afternoon was gone.

Eventually, Nicole herded her daughters to the door. "I'm so sorry we never got a chance to meet Jay, but it couldn't have been more wonderful to meet you…and to see where Lisa grew up…and you made such a wonderful dinner…."

Ann listened to all that blah blah blah, standing at the door, nodding…until Jay's car suddenly pulled in the drive. Immediately the whole crew had to meet Jay, go through the whole rigmarole again of handshaking and smiles and all that to-do. Jay looked wiped out to beat the band, but he did his courtesy thing, extending it as long as Nicole seemed to want to chat.

And Nicole *did* seem to want to chat. She sidled up to Jay as if maybe they could or should have made a couple children themselves. Ann found her gaze narrowing, disbelieving the hip-shifting, eye-flashing moves the woman was putting on right in front of her daughters. With a married man. In front of Ann. *And* Lisa.

Okay, Ann admitted to herself, since no one else seemed to notice Nicole's inappropriate flirting behavior, it was possible—a *little* possible—that her emotions were just slightly frayed by that point in the evening.

Finally her crew were free to head back in the house. Dusk was falling by the time they closed the door. "You have to be starving, Jay," Ann said.

"I am. Last couple hours, all I could think about was that terrific dinner of yours. How'd it all go, you two?"

While Ann heaped a feast on a plate for Jay, Lisa took over the recap. "It couldn't have been better in a thousand years, Dad. Everybody had a good time, except for not having a chance to meet you. But Nicole loved Mom, naturally. So did the girls. It was so funny, how... And Nicole said..."

Ann felt Jay's gaze on her, even as he listened and responded to their daughter. And she kept shooting him pumped-up smiles, determined to show him that he'd been dead wrong about this dinner—which was mostly the truth. It had been good for Lisa.

And she'd handled it just fine. Piece-of-cake fine. No-sweat fine.

Jay settled at the table with his steaming plate, and Lisa took her usual perch next to him—with another serving of Apple Kuchen, although heaven only knew where she was going to put it. Ann brought up the rear with a mug of tea.

Lisa kept on with another set of "Nicole said" and "Nicole..." before she suddenly paused, and then blurted out, "She told me something."

"What?" Jay asked, obviously as aware as Ann that there was something different in Lisa's tone.

"About my birth dad. When we first met she said she'd fill me in on the rest of the story but she never did. Maybe because the girls were always around. But while we were in the kitchen doing dishes and Mom had the girls cornered in the living room, she just kind of spilled it out." Lisa shrugged, like it didn't matter.

Ann exchanged a quick glance with Jay. They both knew that shrug meant it *did* matter.

"Anyway…" Lisa jumped to her feet to pour a fresh glass of milk. "His name was Steve. I guess he was, like, the class jock. The football star. Big man at the high school level. Nicole said she fell for him just like all the other girls did."

"So what happened?" Jay said.

"She slept with him. Then found out he'd been making his way down the cheerleaders. She was, like, the seventh. That she knew of. Only nobody else was dumb enough to get pregnant—or that's how she put it. On the other hand…." Lisa took a long gulp, and then swiped off her milk moustache as she sat down again. "…apparently the next two girls got STD's. Which she didn't. You know what?"

Since she directed the question to her dad, Ann didn't have to answer. She just watched the play of expressive emotions in her daughter's face.

"What?" Jay asked obediently.

"When Nicole was telling me this…I think she wanted to confess how stupid she'd been. At least that's how it came across. Like she wanted me to know she'd been…gullible, but that wasn't the same as being promiscuous or wild. It seemed important to her that I believe she hadn't slept around. She really thought she loved the guy. Only…."

When Lisa didn't immediately follow through with the comment, Ann asked, "Only what, honey?"

"Only she was kind of making the story all about her. Which it was, I guess. But I was thinking about me. Because I wanted to know what kind of birth dad I had. So…at first I felt this huge let-down because my birth father was such a jerk. And a little scared that I'd have his creepy genes. But then…." She took a breath and smiled at Jay. "Then I just got happy again. Because *you're* my dad. Not him. I totally lucked out in the dad department, so what's to complain, you know?"

Jay said to Ann, "She's going to hit me up for a new car, I just know it."

That made Lisa laugh and swing her arms around his neck. They tussled, father-daughter style, until Ann finally banished them from the kitchen. But she was chuckling, too, as she scooped up the last of the dishes and fed them to the dishwasher. There was just a moment, as she gave the counters one last swipe and switched off the kitchen light, when Lisa's reaction to information about her birth father sank in.

Jay couldn't doubt that he was a terrific parent. Still, it had to be extra affirming for him to know that Lisa had found out about her birth dad, yet she would choose Jay for her dad any day of the week.

Ann started walking toward the den to join the family, when she suddenly stopped in the dark. A thick lump clogged her throat. Her eyes suddenly burned so fiercely that she could hardly see.

She and Jay had been lucky enough to choose their

daughter…but their daughter had never had the opportunity to choose her own parents. Finding out about her birth parents seemed to offer revelations for everyone. For darn sure, Lisa had discovered that she'd have picked Jay for her father if she'd had the choice.

But she was getting along so well with Nicole. She'd gotten sisters out of this deal. Gotten to see how much she looked like Nicole. And God knew, Ann loved her and—*really*—was certain that Lisa loved her right back. There was nothing new there. Nothing taken away. Nothing destroyed.

It was just…if Lisa could have chosen a mother, Ann wasn't sure which one she'd have picked.

Jay was standing at the nurses' desk, just signing off on charts before going home, when he heard Martha Rae—the day supervisor on third—talking to one of the other nurses. "I understand you'd like the day off for Mother's Day. But so does everyone else. You know how holidays go. Maybe you can find someone who'll trade shifts for you, like someone who really wants July 4 off."

He tackled Martha Rae a few moments later. "When's Mother's Day?"

She looked at him with the condescending, patient look she gave all the doctors. At least, all the male doctors. "Next Sunday. The second Sunday in May. The same as every year. It's not the same as forgetting an anniversary, but if I were you, I'd pop for flowers just so you don't get in deep trouble."

"How come you didn't remind me before this?"

"Because every year, I keep thinking you men might get a brain."

Jay laughed, but as he took the elevator down to the parking level, his mind was spinning.

Next Sunday. Mother's Day was next Sunday. Only nobody had mentioned it at home…and normally Ann would be all revved up for the occasion. So would Lisa, talking about where they were going to dinner and what they were going to do.

He punched in Ann's cell on the walk to the car.

"You're going to be late for dinner," she said, even before he'd said hello.

"No, smartass. I'm bringing takeout home."

"Oh my God. I'm sending my lover away right now. It's you and me for life."

"Very cute, very cute. But I had a real question—what's on for Sunday?"

"What do you mean?"

He almost stared at the phone, her voice sounded so phony. "I mean, are you and Lisa going off to do something together? Or are we all going out to dinner? Is there a plan?"

"No."

"What do you mean—no?"

"Darn it, Jay, I've got another call coming in—" But she took two seconds to answer his question. "I mean, that I don't know whether she's doing something with Nicole. Or with us. I gather Nicole asked her to do something on Sunday. That's all I've heard. Catch you when you get home."

And then she hung up, using the excuse of the other call.

Jay stood in the middle of the parking lot tarmac until a

car honked at him from behind. The night Nicole had come to dinner, he thought he'd heard Ann crying in the night…but when he'd said her name, she hadn't responded. She'd made out, nonstop, that Lisa's relationship with Nicole was A-OK with her.

But nothing was A-OK. And his wife was more distant from him than ever.

More relevant, she was so damned miserable it was ripping him up.

He glanced at his watch, and then hustled into the car and took off. His mind rollercoasted choices, options. Maybe he should call Lisa. Lisa should know how much her mother was feeling hurt. Only maybe calling Lisa was the worst thing, because Ann didn't want her to know how sensitive she was about Nicole.

Maybe he should do this.

Maybe he should do that.

The bottom line was that the relationship between Ann and Lisa was nothing he really had power over. Not that he could see. What he *could* see was Ann. Her sadness. Her hurt. How the damn woman was wallowing into believing that she wasn't as important to Lisa as before.

Being a mom had been more important to Ann than everything else. Always and forever. And far more important than he'd been to her…but that, for the moment, was neither here nor there.

He couldn't wield a magic scalpel and force the girls to talk to each other.

He couldn't seem to fix their marriage either.

But he did have the power to do a few things. And he was about to wield that power, in spades.

RAIN OR NO RAIN, Ann was planting petunias. She didn't particularly care for gardening, and for darn sure didn't like worms, but it was a tradition, on Mother's Day morning, to spruce up the yard for summer. That meant buying baskets of impatiens for the shady back porch, mixed pots for the deck—and petunias under the front window in the semi-circle framing the arbor vitae. It took a whole flat to do the job.

She liked it when it was done. She just didn't like the dirt and the worms part.

And the raining part.

School was out—and Lisa had been running around like a mad thing since she got home. Job hunting. Creating messes. Moving messes. Creating new messes. Having friends over and making dates with friends and, of course, seeing Nicole and the girls.

She hadn't said a word about Mother's Day, but she'd slept at a friend's last night—or so she'd said. Since she was too old for sleepovers, Ann suspected she'd either stayed at a boy's or at Nicole's.

Either way, Ann hadn't said anything to Lisa. Or to Jay.

But she'd woken up that morning with a hurt so big she could barely swallow, barely think. The drizzle on the windows suited her mood just fine. Without Lisa this year, she'd gone out to buy the flat of flowers, got the spade, the gloves, the kneeling pad and dug in.

She was two-thirds through the job. Rain had drooled down the back of her collar, her toes felt mucky inside her tennies and her back ached to beat the band...when she suddenly heard the front door open. She didn't look up. It had to be Jay. And she should have left a note so Jay knew where she was—even though she was just outside, he wouldn't have known that, wouldn't have known why she wasn't buried in the Sunday paper with coffee the way they did together every Sunday.

But she couldn't talk to Jay right now. Couldn't talk at all.

He didn't say anything, just came up behind her in the drizzle—she could feel him even if she couldn't see his shadow. She just kept on, making wells with the spade, then dunking the baby flowers out of their holes, then loving them in with her hands.

Out of nowhere, it seemed, a spill of pastel Easter eggs showed up on the muddy ground next to her. She glanced up then, because how could she not? They were the kind of little plastic eggs you decorated kids' Easter baskets with when they were little—which was fine. She'd probably had them in the upstairs closet since Lisa was ten. But it was a long time past Easter, and Easter certainly had nothing to do with this Sunday besides.

Jay had on an old sweatshirt and even older khakis, but the expression in his eyes…

She couldn't read it, but something about his eyes looked…young. And new. And different.

"What's with the eggs?"

"I was thinking about creating a new holiday."

"I think it's too late for Easter, honey."

"I know. But all I could find to put surprises in were those eggs. This holiday, I was thinking, was about…well, it was about wives. Because there doesn't seem to be an annual holiday for wives." Suddenly he looked panicked. "Is there?"

"No, you silly." But she was completely confused.

"Like on Easter, you have to crack open the eggs to find out what's in there."

She cracked open an egg. And found a piece of paper that claimed she had a full day at a fancy spa paid for in her name, for the works—seaweed wrap, facial, full body massage and a cosmetic analysis.

"I don't have a clue what 'cosmetic analysis' is, but it came with the package," Jay said.

"Do you have any idea how much that place charges?"

"I do now. It seemed a lot to pay for seaweed, but what do I know? She said it was a guarantee that you'd feel pampered. Open the next one."

She did. Again a slip of paper slid out...this one for a lobster dinner a deux. Not at a restaurant. At a penthouse suite in one of the fanciest hotels in town.

That lump in her throat, the one that was all about Mother's Day, suddenly seemed to have a different name on it. "Jay," she said thickly. "I can't believe this. I don't understand...you didn't have to—"

"You're not finished."

There were three more, but when she reached for the blue plastic egg, he said, "Wait. Do that one last."

So she went for the yellow plastic egg and found a pair of truffles from the Chocolate Garden. Not just her favorite, but her favorite vice from her favorite place.

He said, "No, you don't have to share, they're both for you." And put the pink Easter egg in her hand.

Inside was a check for a thousand dollars. Not to her. But to an organization that rescued abandoned or abused girl children in Middle Eastern countries.

"All right," she said thickly. "I have no idea why you'd be so mean as to make me cry—"

"Just open the last one, Ann."

She did, and found a ring wrapped in a scrap of velvet. It fell out, almost dropped to the damp ground, but she scooped it up in time. When she opened her fist, the stone shone like a rainbow in the heart of her palm. She looked at Jay, speechless, then back at the extraordinary ring.

"I'll tell you what I was thinking." He hunkered down next to her, casual as if they were two kids playing in the dirt together. "We couldn't afford much of a ring for you when we first got married. And then, you've been working with so many troubled, poor kids that I know you'd never want to wear anything too big or ostentatious. Just wouldn't be the right message. But…then I thought…it wasn't the worst message for those kids to see that you were loved. That your guy chose to give you something to make you feel loved. Because you are loved, Ann. More than when we first married. More than ten years ago. More than yesterday. And I'm damned sure I'll love you even more tomorrow."

He leaned forward, took her left hand, and pulled the single gold band from her ring finger—which took some tugging. Then reached for the new ring. The marquise glittered more than sunlight, more than rainbows.

She lifted her eyes to him, tears welling so thick she struggled to speak. She saw Jay every day. Loved him. Thought of him as part of her life, as her shadow. He was her husband, her mate.

But it had been a long time since she'd looked at him solely as a man. As her lover.

The crinkles around his eyes hadn't been there when they first married. His hair had been thicker. But he still had that dark-eyed gaze that made her feel weak at the knees. He still had that mouth that she wanted to own. He still had that look…that tall, lean, loner look…that made her want to wrap her arms around him and take him into her life where no one could hurt him and she could love the loneliness right out of him.

How had she forgotten those feelings?

Here they were, just like yesterday, only more. So much more. And she'd just been looking past him, looking past her own heart and feelings, as if they were an irrelevant part of their every-day.

"Jay," she said in a fierce, urgent whisper…only before she could say anything further, a car pulled in the drive.

Lisa tumbled out of the car with a door slam and a shriek. "MOM! What are you DOING? You KNOW we do the petunias together every Mother's Day!!"

Jay laughed, and so, suddenly did Ann. They both got to their feet at the same time—and both seemed to realize the misty drizzle was threatening to turn into a deluge. She scooped up her eggs and they peeled toward the house, all three of them reaching the back door at the same time.

Lisa was still talking. "I need you to sit down in the den and close your eyes. No arguing with me. No guessing—"

Ann kept looking at Jay, wanting to talk to him, to say the things she was suddenly desperate to say—only their daughter was clearly in a bouncy, exuberant, determined-to-monopolize-them-both kind of mood. And it WAS Mom's Day, so she could hardly shut Lisa out, not that she'd ever want to do that anyway. "I didn't know if we were doing Mother's Day," she said.

"Huh? Why would you think otherwise?"

"Well," Ann said, "I just thought you'd feel pulled, toward spending the day here or with Nicole. And I—"

"You can't be serious, Mom. For Pete's sake. I was an egg to her she didn't want. I'm not her daughter. She isn't my mom." Lisa laughed at such a silly nothing, and came over to buss Ann on both cheeks. "I've been gone quite a bit lately—"

"I know."

"And I've told you a few times I was hanging with Nicole."

"I know."

"Well, it was a lie. I was at a friend's. But I didn't want you to know that because I was making you something for Mom's Day. And that's why I didn't come home last night. I stayed up late to finish it, but when I finally did I crashed and didn't wake up until a bit ago. Now. WOULD you—and Dad—go sit in the den and close your eyes?"

"Hey, why do I have to close my eyes?" Jay complained.

"Are you kidding? I can't trust you to keep a secret from Mom. Even for a second. There. Sit." Like a pint-sized general, she used the royal finger to order them together on the couch. "Close your eyes. Tight. No peeking."

They did. Tight. No peeking. But in those few seconds before Lisa produced the mysterious Mother's Day present, Ann groped next to her for Jay's hand. Found it.

Slid her fingers between his and held tight.

"Ta da!"

Huffing and puffing, Lisa carried in a screen—a room divider screen, the kind that folded up and could be put out of sight, or could be used as a privacy barrier. Each panel was a collage of photographs, some black and white, some color, all shellacked and preserved.

"I made it, Mom. I used a friend's tools to cut the wood and make the frames. Then had a friend help me figure out the hinges. Then I varnished the wood. Then I had to find all the photographs from boxes where you wouldn't likely look…and, I admit, I don't know if you'll ever find a use for it. I guess it's pretty worthless. But I was trying to make you something personal, something that was really about Mother's Day, you know— Mom! I can't breathe!"

But Lisa, laughing, hugged Ann back as hard as Ann was hugging her. "I can't think of a gift in the world that's more thoughtful for Mother's Day, you darling." Ann pulled back, then crouched by the screen again, studying each picture with Lisa right next to her.

"Remember that one? When we went to the beach and I buried myself in sand and couldn't move?"

"You thought you couldn't get out," Ann said with a chuckle.

"And this one. Dad shot this, didn't you, Dad? When we were making shaving cream pictures with food coloring.

Took out the whole kitchen table and the floor, but didn't we have fun?"

"I can't believe you can remember back that far."

"Oh, yeah, I remember. And I remember this Mother's Day picture, when I made you scrambled eggs in the microwave and brought you breakfast in bed."

"Oh my God. You were so proud. And the eggs were so awful."

"But you ate them."

"Of course I ate them. You made them for me."

"Remember this one? My first day at school. I loved that dress."

"That was your purple year. You didn't want to wear anything that wasn't purple...."

Lisa turned to her. "You like it, don't you? The screen?"

"I couldn't love it more in a million, zillion years!"

"Whew. I had fun doing it. But then I started thinking, what on earth are you going to do with the screen? I was afraid it would just get in your way—"

"It'll never get in my way. I can think of all kinds of places for it." Ann suddenly remembered something. "Lisa...I have something for you, too."

"For me? Why? What?"

She'd forgotten about it. The pendant she had for Lisa, strung on a black silk cord, with the engraving. She hustled upstairs, hustled back down.

Lisa opened the case and slowly read the message, Never Forget For A Single Minute…You Didn't Grow Under My Heart—But In It." She lifted tear-filled eyes. "Aw, Mom."

"Don't you start," Ann said, but she snuggled her arms around her daughter with misty eyes, too. "I thought of you the minute I saw it. Happy Mother's Day, daughter."

"Happy Mother's Day, Mom. I love you so much!"

"Okay, I can't take much more of this." Jay stood up, shaking his head. "If you two are going to cry, I'm either going to hide in the basement…or take you both out for a lobster dinner."

A lobster dinner it was, although they had to wait in line for an eternity…on the other hand, the females didn't mind, because they talked nonstop anyway. Hours later, Jay carted the two women home, both moaning from overeating and claiming they'd never eat again. He suffered through a chick flick—the inevitable end to a Mother's Day—and heard the whole round of "thank yous" and "I love its" all over again.

Ann was well aware of his suffering. Mother's Days were always quiet days for him, because he made a point of stepping back.

But she hadn't realized before…how much he'd stepped back. How quiet he'd gotten. With her. Around her.

When the group finally called it a night, it was after eleven. Ann climbed into bed before Jay. He usually stayed up a few moments later, was used to finding his way into a dark bedroom…but this time she was still wide awake.

This time, when he slid into bed, soundless as a secret, she murmured, "Turn on your back."

"Pardon?"

She ignored the rhetorical question. He'd heard her. And she wanted to think that she'd heard him today—the way she hadn't listened in a long, long time. Too long.

Slowly, softly, she drew lines on his back, into his nape, into his scalp, using her fingertips and her palms. "I wanted to show Lisa all the presents you got me. But first…I wanted to thank you. Alone. Just you and me. Because they weren't about Lisa, they were about us, weren't they?"

Normally she'd have let him answer. But when she stroked his scalp just so, invariably the only sound his vocal cords could produce were groans.

"I love the ring, Jay."

She rubbed and kept rubbing. Making two fists, then gently rolling her fists down his vertebrae on each side, then kneading outward. Eliciting more painful groans.

"I love all the other presents, too. Each one was so special, so thoughtful. Each one was so…loving."

He'd never lasted as long on a backrub as she did, partly because he'd always turned on faster than the flip of a dime. But this night, dark or no dark, he turned around and drew her onto his chest. She could see the dark gleam in his eyes, the tenderness, the…quiet.

"Ann," he started to say.

But she interrupted him. Not because she didn't want to hear him, but because she knew she would be careful to listen from now on. And there were a few things she still needed to say.

"I felt like an outsider when she found Nicole. You knew I did. But I couldn't admit it." Since she had new territory to play with, she took advantage, prowling and stroking his chest. Chest, neck, chin, temples. "It was about feeling like a trespasser in her life, Jay. Feeling like a trespasser in yours. If I did things for you, with you, and just kind of stayed invisible otherwise, then you'd never know it. That I was an imposter. An outsider."

"Where," he whispered, "did you ever get such a damn fool idea?"

She didn't hesitate with her touch. But she did in her heart. "I'm not sure. But I think it was when I found out I couldn't have children. I felt like less of a woman. Not just because I couldn't be a mother. But also…less of a woman with you."

"Damn it, Ann," he said lowly, "why couldn't you have told me how you felt?"

"Because…I didn't have a name for it. I didn't KNOW. It was just a feeling of not belonging anymore." Somehow she found her back on the mattress, his leaning over her, just like…just like the first time he'd first made love to her. He had that same burnished gleam in his gaze, the same intensity, the same rough tumble of hair in the moonlight.

"You're everything in this family. Everything to me."

"I belong," she said. "To you. With you. I get it now. Really, really get it."

She meant it. It wasn't the presents, the material gifts, that opened her eyes. It was his thinking of her...his thinking about what she needed and wanted. It was realizing that he'd been quietly thinking of her, loving her, without her being aware for a long time.

She lifted up, to offer the first kiss of the night...but not the last.

When she was young, she thought being in love was everything a woman could wish for...that growing older with a man would be dull and take all the sizzle out of it.

It wasn't the first thing she'd been wrong about.

But picking this man to love and be loved by...she'd never been wrong about that, and she showed him how she felt in loving, enthusiastic detail throughout the night.

* * * * *

Watch for a brand new story from Jennifer Greene, coming soon from Harlequin Next.

BECOMING MY MOTHER, AND OTHER THINGS I LEARNED FROM JANE AUSTEN

NANCY ROBARDS THOMPSON

From the Author

Dear Reader,

Most of us, at one point or another, will experience that breath-stealing moment when we realize that, like it or not, we have become our mother.

We may hear her in an uttered phrase or catch a surprise glimpse of her in our reflection. No matter how it happens, it seems that all our lives we've been journeying toward the very moment of "Oh, my gosh, I've become my mother."

Maybe that's not such a bad thing….

In my story "Becoming My Mother, and Other Things I Learned from Jane Austen," the heroine, Esme, finally draws that conclusion after years of struggling to be the polar opposite of her mom, Georgia. In the process, Esme learns that the journey toward love begins with a few small steps of acceptance.

Why not take this moment to tell your mother or the mother figure in your life how much she means to you?

Warmly,

Nancy Robards Thompson

This book is dedicated to my four mothers:

Barbara Robards, whose time on this earth
was much too short, but while she
was here had a profound influence on my life;
Lynn Robards—I couldn't have handpicked
a better mother than you;
Wiladean Barnett, who was more like a
mother than a grandma, but still a terrific grandma.
Oh, how I miss you; and
Juanita Eitreim—How did I get so lucky to have
such a wonderful mother-in-law?

Each of you means the world to me, and I love you dearly.

"Twenty years from now you will be more disappointed by the things that you didn't do than by the ones you did do. So throw off the bowlines. Sail away from the safe harbor. Catch the trade winds in your sails. Explore. Dream. Discover." —Mark Twain

DAY 1

8:46 a.m.

A little voice inside me always insists I color within the lines. I heed it because that's just who I am. It's the way I'm built. Perhaps it stems from an overriding need to be the polar opposite of my mother, Georgia Valentine-Boroughs-Stanley-Gaines-English, who'd refined scribbling outside the lines to a fine art.

I've watched her break rules for as long as I've been aware of right and wrong. Of course, she never did anything illegal. Just little white lies and manipulations—all performed with a smile on her pretty face and a twinkle in her wide hazel eyes.

We get along fine when there's an ocean between us. My mother lives in Florida with hubby number five. I make my home in London, and for the interim in Paris, as I'm expanding my company, Valentine Tours, into France.

We offer an array of excursions that bring favorite books to life. Our slogan is "Why just read a book when you can walk in the footsteps of your favorite literary character?" In London, the favorites are tours featuring sights in Jane Austen novels: picnics on Box Hill à la *Emma*, readings from *Persuasion* along the quay in Lyme Regis, Chatsworth House in Derbyshire—better known to *Pride and Prejudice* addicts as Mr. Darcy's Pemberley.

It's all so bloody romantic.

People will shell out big bucks to be swept away by a little romance. I'm more than happy to collect their money.

My grandmother used to read me Jane Austen stories. So I guess they're imprinted in my soul.

But I'll be honest; I was ready for a change. I woke up one sad morning sick of the romance.

It was like eating too much chocolate.

Chocolate is delicious, but no one can tolerate a steady diet of it. So, I left the Austen tours in the capable hands of my London associates and escaped to Paris to do a tour based on *The Da Vinci Code*.

More intrigue. Less romance. For the past six months, it's made my loveless, business-focused life seem less pathetic, and the new challenge swept me away.

But I digress; I was talking about my relationship with my mother.

We have a love-hate relationship, she and I. It stems from issues that reach way back—such as how after my father died when I was ten years old, she was too busy dating to raise me, so she dumped me on my father's mother.

It wasn't an altogether bad arrangement. My grandmother and I were soul mates in the platonic sense of the word. She gave me a good upbringing. But just as I'd be getting in the flow, my mother would start thinking she was settled with one of her various husbands and pluck me out of my grandmother's house to come live with her.

She always gave me back—when motherhood got too hard or too inconvenient. When I got a little older and the men started looking at me in that certain way…

I'm not pulling the poor-me card or playing the victim, and I'm certainly not blaming my personal issues on my mother. I don't believe in that. Because even though the past has some effect on the psyche, I think the onus lies on each individual to pull herself up and out of the mire. So like I said, I don't blame her, I just don't want to be like her.

Good thing, because my mother and I *really* are total opposites. I'm a workaholic. She's had a series of "between men" jobs, each of which she ditched once the new husband started supporting her.

I love her. I do. In my own way. Even though I can't

remember us saying the words to each other since my father died nearly twenty-five years ago.

Still, I love her because…well, that's just what you do. You love your mother. I'm not necessarily cognizant of it as I go through my daily routine; my feelings for her—good or bad—don't loom in the back of my mind like a phantom. She's just my mother and it would feel…un-American not to love her. Even though I'm an expat, I'm still an American through and through.

But just because she's my mother, that doesn't mean I have to *like* her and her shenanigans.

That's why, on the first day of our third *Da Vinci Code* tour, I should've smelled a rat.

My business partner, Raoul Leon, and I stood in the Salon Cambon of the Paris Ritz Hotel stalling for time as we waited on one late arrival, whose name was—get this—*Venus D. Milo.*

When Raoul told me the client's name, I thought he was joking. For a split second I wondered if perhaps our office assistant, Solange, made a mistake. Her grasp of English worked on a sliding scale of good (when she was booking reservations—most of which came from English-speaking men who wanted to make the tour part of their bigger vacation picture) all the way down to horrific (when it came to certain office policies she found unnecessary or unpalatable).

Maybe it was her idea of a joke?

However, since Solange didn't seem to own a sense of humor—or anything remotely resembling one—I had no choice but to assume that Ms. *Venus D. Milo* must be a real flesh and blood, paying client whose parents were cruel enough to saddle their child with an unfortunate name.

My name, Esmeralda, is enough of a clunker that I shortened it to Esme. But Ms. Milo definitely gets the awkward moniker prize.

Ritz servers were clearing the trays of croissants and pastries and tiding up the room. I was getting a little panicked because we were already off schedule, and Raoul insisted we give this Ms. Milo ten more minutes. He said he'd called the Hôtel du Carrousel, where the clients were staying. She had, indeed, checked in late last night, despite not arriving in time to catch the group transfer from Charles de Gaulle Airport.

I sensed she had punctuality problems, which I did not care to indulge. Still, I decided to trust Raoul, who was perfectly at ease waiting for her, and, I must admit, looking particularly handsome in his dark suit and green tie that brought out the color of his eyes.

From the moment a mutual friend had introduced us, he'd reminded me of someone. It took me a few days to realize, with his olive skin and dark hair, he bore a striking resemblance to Johnny Depp with short hair—except taller, larger boned and undeniably French.

From the moment we started talking business, I made the decision that any personal attraction I might feel for him must take a back seat to business. In no time at all, he became my "French connection," serving as concierge, translator and general problem solver, paving the way as we lead clients on tour.

What would I do without him? I remind myself every time a rogue feeling breaks free of the compartment in which I've safely stashed it. Thank God that only happens occasionally. Like the times I catch him looking at me in a certain way that can send me into a tailspin if I don't get my act together and compartmentalize my emotions—and fast.

So on this day of the rat, Raoul was on the phone confirming our lunch reservation and explaining we might be a little late. To distract myself from the seconds of tardiness ticking into minutes, I opened my folder to review the day's itinerary. There's nothing like Paris in late May. Perfect walking weather.

So, first we'd take a short walk to the Arc de Triomphe du Carrousel that Napoleon I had erected to commemorate France's military victories. From there we'd walk the length of the Jardin des Tuileries, that splendid expanse of park that stretches from the Louvre to the Place de la Concorde, where the bus would pick us up and drive us down the Champs-Élysées to the Arc de Triomphe.

Next we'd drive over to the Gare Saint-Lazare; past the

Opera Garnier, Paris' world-famous opera house; over to La Madeleine, with its Marochetti statue of Mary Magdalene being carried up to heaven by two angels; we'd break for lunch; and finally finish the day exploring Notre Dame Cathedral on the Île de la Cité. The clients would enjoy dinner on their own, and we would reconvene at 8:00 p.m. for a trip to the Champs de Mars to view the Eiffel Tower light show before calling it a night.

"They will still accommodate us as long as we're not more than an hour late. After that—"

He broke off as a whirlwind of a woman blew into the small room, all flowing scarves, sweeping skirt, clanking bracelets and clattering high heels.

"I'm here! I'm here! Thank God you didn't leave without me."

Raoul clapped. "Ah! *Bonjour, madame*. Ladies and gentlemen, may I present our missing Venus D. Milo."

Mother? What the— "This is *not* Venus D. Milo," I said to Raoul. "This is my mother."

I clutched my folder, fearing she'd break into song, delivering a rousing rendition of *I'm Your Venus*. That would have been just like her. Instead, she ran over, heels clacking on the parquet floor, and threw her arms around me in an uncharacteristic display of tenderness toward me.

"Oh, my darlin'! I am so glad to see you."

I was floored not only by my mother's impromptu appearance but also by the fact that she was hugging me. Since my father's funeral, I honestly can't remember another time she's embraced me. Physically or emotionally. It was as if something inside of her broke when he died.

She pulled away and looked me over from head to toe. "Esme, I thought you would have gotten a fancy Parisian makeover by now." She shook her head, and I detected a note of disappointment in her expression. "Well, that's okay. You always did march to your own basic drum."

I ran an unmanicured hand through my straight, brown bob, pondering a good comeback to her backhanded compliment. Beauty was another category in which my mother and I were diametrically opposed. She was beautiful. I was—err—rather plain, as Jane Austen would have said. Thank goodness Raoul appeared and changed the subject.

"You are finally here," he said.

Mom beamed. "You must be Raoul. Thank you for helping me surprise my daughter."

"*Enchanté*, madame."

As they kissed each other on both cheeks like old friends, I shifted from one foot to the next in my sensible low-heeled black pumps, staring at my mother's strappy sandals thinking, if she's taking this tour, those sexy shoes are completely inappropriate. For as far back as I could remember, my mother had never cared about something so inconsequential as being appropriate. That was no fun.

So I turned my irritation on Raoul. "You knew about this?"

He looked entirely too proud of himself. "*Oui*."

My mother cleared her throat.

"Esmeralda, you didn't tell me your *business partner*," she put air quotes around business partner, "was so charmin'. It's about time you got yourself a man. If you want to call him a *business partner* you go right ahead, sweetie. Sex is the only kind of business I ever had any interest in anyway."

A vision of making love with Raoul flashed across the movie screen of my mind. Heat spread across my face like wildfire, and I couldn't look at him. Instead, I glanced around the room to see if any of the other clients were listening. Some were within earshot, but most were finishing their coffee and croissants.

I squeezed my eyes closed for a moment, trying to erase the mental picture of Raoul. Surely, this was a bad dream. I would wake up soon and breathe a sigh of relief when I discovered my mother had not signed up for my tour and she was not spouting off sexual innuendos about my relationship with Raoul. When I opened my eyes, she was still there.

Eyeing Raoul, she said to me, "I'm glad to see you're finally waking up after the disaster with Kyle. He was an idiot and not nearly as handsome as Raoul here."

Kyle was my former fiancé. The one and only time mother met him was at my grandmother's funeral, five years ago. In fact, that was the last time I'd seen my mother. But we pretended to keep in touch with our once-a-month phone calls, which is how she knew that Kyle and I were no longer together. Though it hardly gave her the right to call him an idiot, even if that's exactly what he was.

Raoul knew all about Kyle. In fact, we'd confided in each other, exchanging relationship war stories when his relationship with his long-time girlfriend was on the rocks. They eventually broke up and have been apart for three months now.

Even though Raoul knew all about me, there was something mortifying about my mother dredging up the biggest relationship failure in my life.

I had to get this situation under control before she did any more damage.

"If you'll excuse us for a moment," I said to Raoul, making a mental note to talk to him about his keeping this surprise visit from me.

"Come with me." I grabbed my mother by the arm and led her out the French doors onto the terrace overlooking the beautiful Jardin César Ritz.

She shook free of my grasp. "Esmeralda, there's no need to get your panties in a wad. It's just sex. Raoul's a gorgeous man. There's nothing to be ashamed of."

That little piece of me that didn't die when we were inside gasped for breath as we stood on the patio. Would I ever be able to look Raoul in the eyes again? Would my clients ever be able to take me seriously with my mother on this tour? Not if I let her swoop in and ruin everything I'd worked so hard to build.

"Mother, I—err—Raoul is my friend and business partner. I am *not* sleeping with him. And if I were, it would be none of your business." I gritted my teeth. "*What* are you doing here?"

She arched a brow and crossed her arms, leaning away from me ever so slightly. "I'm taking your tour. I paid for it in full. So I do hope you'll show me the same respect you offer the others."

She paused and let the words dangle in the air, their sharp edges virtually gleaming in the soft, morning light. Despite her free-spirited nature, she had a quick temper and a sharp wit that always sidelined me.

Today, I was not prepared to go to the mat. Not when twenty-four other people expected me to deliver my best. Several travel agents were giving the tour a test run. Word of mouth was one of the biggest factors as to whether a tour sprouted wings or tanked. To get the buzz going, I had to put on a spectacular show. I hate to admit I was relieved to see a slow smile spread over her face.

"Besides, someone has a birthday this week." She sang the words. "I wanted to surprise you, Miss Stuffy Pants. So, surprise!"

Oh, great. My birthday. Honestly, I'd put it out of my mind.

I found it hard to believe she'd really dropped everything to surprise me for my birthday. Especially when most of my life she'd been too wrapped up in her own affairs to remember something so trivial.

"Well, that certainly is a surprise," I finally managed. "Where's Dr. Benny?"

Or was it Benji? No, wait. It was Benny. Benji was husband number three. He was a good man, actually, but she traded him in as if she were at the end of an auto lease and wanted to trade up. She couldn't wait to get her hands on a newer, more expensive model.

She stiffened and smoothed her hair. Something in the air between us shifted.

"He's back in Florida." She turned in a slow circle, spreading her arms wide. "I can not believe I'm in Paris for my baby's birthday. Look at this view. Oh, just breathe in that air. That's Paris air. And that room in there." She gestured to the Salon Cambon. Through the glass, I could see Raoul engaging the other clients. He was so good at that. I felt confident he'd be able to charm them into forgetting my mother's grand entrance. If anyone could put a spin on it, he could.

"And look at this garden," my mother said. "This is the life. Maybe I'll just move here."

She smiled at me, and despite my better judgment, the little girl inside me smiled at the thought of her coming all this way by herself just to see me.

For *me*. On my birthday.

"Would Benny move here?"

It was a ridiculous question. They weren't moving here. But conversations with my mother usually went one of two ways—strained and stilted or bordering on the absurd. So why not…

She acted as if she didn't hear me. "I always thought the mama should get a present on her baby's birthday since she's the one responsible for bringing the little darlin' into the world in the first place."

She sighed. "Since I'm the mama, I'm giving myself Paris for your birthday."

Okay, so maybe her being here wasn't *all* for me. This was one of those glass half-empty or half-full moments. I decided, that since she'd made the effort to be here, the glass was half-full.

"We are going to have the time of our lives, baby girl. I'll make sure of it."

The time of our lives? Oh, boy.

Movement by the French doors caught my eye, and I turned to see Raoul motioning to us.

"We are ready to leave," he said.

If he could pretend my mother hadn't been talking about me having sex with him just minutes ago, I could meet him halfway. Still, the image of making love to him flashed in my mind again. I blinked it away.

"We'll be right there." A gentle spring breeze blew across the terrace. "If you're serious about taking this tour, Mom, we need to get going. We're late."

She brushed her bangs out of her eyes. "Well, let's get this show on the road then."

As we followed the others into the lobby, I whispered. "Venus de Milo, Mother? *Seriously.*"

She smiled like Alice's Cheshire cat.

"At least I didn't come in topless. Of course, if going topless is *de rigueur*, I say when in Paris, do as the Romans do…."

Her voice carried, and to my horror, at least two women pulled their husbands closer.

I rolled my eyes. "Well thank God we're not planning a beach trip."

She gave my arm a little push and clucked her tongue. In my mind, I took out the big, fat black Sharpie I used to cross off items on my mental to-do list and lined through *possible beach trip for tour?*

"Oh, I'm in Paris and I'm just giddy over it," she said as we caught up with Raoul at the hotel's front door. "You see, Raoul, I thought Venus de Milo was so French. That's why I used her as my cover."

"Actually, she's Greek," he said, injecting an extra dose of charm. If I could have caught his eye, I would have made a face at him. "The Aphrodite of Milos was her original name. She was discovered in 1820 by a Greek peasant named Yorgos Kentrotas on the island of Milos. A French naval officer recognized her significance and arranged for purchase by the French government. That is how the lady came to France."

My mother eyed Raoul and said in her best stage whisper, "Not only is he sexy, the guy's smart, too."

Raoul smiled, lured by her siren song. A strange note of protectiveness flared inside me.

He had no idea who he was dealing with.

"You're married, Mother. Raoul, she's *married*."

She waved off my words. "Pfffft. Not for much longer. He dumped me."

11:00 a.m.

IN THE PAST MY mother always did the dumping, littering the way with a trail of brokenhearted casualties. That morning, I didn't have time to grill her for the details of the Benny debacle because I had to give my tour spiel about how each of the landmarks along the way related to the book. Still, I pondered her being on the receiving end of the breakup for a change, half expecting the sky to fall.

As we walked, I saw her cozying up to Raoul.

I realized in horror that if she'd dumped hubby number five, according to her MO, she'd be primed and ready to get her red manicured claws into hubby number six. And over my dead body would Raoul be my new stepfather.

To make it worse, he was flirting back. I could *not* believe he was flirting back.

He said something to her in a low voice.

She tittered and her raspy, southern, "Why, Raoul, I'm charmed," carried across the distance.

I wanted to roll my eyes, but I couldn't since the guests were asking me questions.

He said something else and they both laughed.

That protectiveness I'd felt earlier turned inside out, sprouting horns and fangs, morphing into something ugly.

Doing my best to keep the beast down, I walked over to them and said, "Raoul, I could use some help explaining some of the *Jardin des Tuileries* landmarks." I exaggerated the accent.

Raoul shot me a puzzled glance, his green-eyed gaze locking with mine. Then he nodded and turned to my mother.

"If you'll excuse me, *madame*, duty calls."

I wished I knew French for, "Save yourself. Run! Run far, far away from that woman."

Alas, I hadn't been studying French long enough to venture beyond the basics.

"What a charming man," my mother said as she watched him walk across the grass to the other clients. As she started to follow him, I reached out and took hold of her arm.

"Mother, wait a minute."

She stopped and flinched out of my grasp.

"I'm not quite sure why you're here…." All of a sudden, words bubbled up and spilled out before I could stop them. "But this tour is my business. Raoul is my business partner.

Just as you asked me to afford you the same respect I show my other clients, I'm asking you to respect my situation."

She narrowed her eyes as if she were aiming a barbed word at my heart, but then she nodded and we walked silently to catch up with the others.

Finally, as we reached the bus at the Place de la Concorde, pausing so the others could board, I said, "So Dr. Benny left?"

"Oooh, you would not believe the hell that man's put me through. I'm finished with men. Period."

Forlorn displacement wrinkled her brow. For a moment I was afraid she'd cry. I didn't know what to say since *Now you know how it feels to get dumped* and *Karma* seemed highly inappropriate. Even if she was getting a taste of her own bitter medicine, I couldn't be that mean.

Not to mention, we had to get on the bus and I had to narrate the rest of the tour. Who knows how far the conversation would've digressed if I'd gone there.

Raoul was already on the bus, checking off names to make sure we didn't leave anyone behind. When the last person boarded, Mom and I ducked into the front seat opposite Raoul. The driver shut the doors, and the show was officially on the road.

Even though I felt bad for my mother, I needed to put on my game face.

"I'm really sorry. I know this must be hard for you."

She nodded solemnly.

"I don't mean to be insensitive, but can we talk about it later? I really need to get to work." I gestured discreetly toward the back of the bus with the microphone. Dabbing at her eyes, she turned around and looked.

She sighed like the drama queen I knew and waved me off. "Oh, of course. Enough about me and my silly problems. I came here to forget men. To start over."

Forget men? Right. For how long?

"Oh, don't look at me like that, Esmeralda. I'm finished with men. I mean it." She crossed her arms over her ample breasts. "Now get to work. Don't keep those people waitin'. It's rude."

"Yes it is rude." I shouldn't have said it. I could've kicked myself, but the words were out before I could stop them. "So promise me you'll be on time for the rest of the week, okay?"

Raoul gave me a what-are-you-doing look, which I'll admit I deserved.

Indignation colored my mother's face. "I am sorry I kept you waiting this mornin'." Her words were crisp and pointed. Then a look passed over her and she got to her feet. "Everybody! Excuse me! May I have your attention please?"

"Mother, no—"

The bus fell silent.

"I am *so* sorry I held everyone up this morning. I just wanted to let you know it was all my fault, not my daughter's. She owns this tour thing-a-ma-jig. She and Raoul were nice enough to wait for me because I was late. With the jet lag and all, I just couldn't get it in gear this morning." She slanted a glance at me. "I just want to assure you it will never happen again."

Oh. My. God. Acutely aware of every eye trained on her, I wanted to melt into the seat.

In all fairness, how could people not look at her? She's gorgeous. Tall and slim, with curves in all the right places. Big hazel eyes and curly golden-brown hair that hangs to her shoulders. Age only seemed to enhance her beauty. And her audacity.

My mother has always been a difficult woman. Albeit, a difficult woman who resembles Susan Sarandon. So she's gotten away with it all her life.

At that moment I, who'd inherited my father's good business sense and less than remarkable looks, probably bore a striking likeness to a church mouse who desperately wanted to scurry away as my mother commanded the pulpit.

I had to take charge of the situation. I tugged on her arm, her cue to sit down.

"Thank you, Mother. You're forgiven."

I stood just as she dropped into the seat and I dropped the microphone.

"*Merde.*" The word slipped out under my breath as I bent to pick up the microphone. Thank God it wasn't on.

"Merde?" My mother cocked her head to the side. "What does that mean?"

"It means *shit*, Mother," I whispered.

"Oh!" She did her best to pretend she was still mad at me, but I could see the grin she was having a hard time suppressing. "Potty mouth."

Finally, I stood and switched on the microphone, trying to ignore the sinking feeling that upon arrival, my mother had jumped out of Pandora's box.

7:30 a.m.

Funny how the power of suggestion can change the way you see someone. Once an idea is planted in the subconscious, it has a way of growing roots and blossoming in that place in your soul that once was the equivalent of unturned earth.

Yesterday, Mother's spouting off about my relationship with Raoul rooted in my subconscious and sprouted a dream about him.

Or should I say, about *us.*

In frightfully vivid, frightfully bad, three-dimensional Technicolor.

Raoul is my friend. What's more, I *never* let the lines between my professional and personal life blur. Although, judging by the dream, you'd never know it. It disturbed me on so many levels because the symbolism was so painfully obvious. It's embarrassing to retell it.

But here goes—

In the dream, Raoul was a Mr. Darcy-type character to my Elizabeth Bennet. We made love at Pemberley.

Do I really have to explain what it all means?

It's simple. If this tour doesn't get off the ground, it's very likely the French leg of Valentine Tours will fold for the foreseeable future. I desperately need Raoul to help keep the venture afloat. Not that it would be impossible without him. But it would be *très difficile*.

Oh, how I hate depending on people. But I'm practical enough to know that going it alone in Paris would be harder than trusting someone else.

So when my friend, Marie, introduced me to Raoul because he had experience working with tourists—he made a nice living managing a consortium of apartments, renting to visitors who wanted a taste of Paris they couldn't get in a hotel—I knew right away he was my man.

He had the vision I was looking for; knew the city; had established contacts; and wasn't afraid to take risks.

I recognized those qualities right away, but I had such tunnel vision when it came to business—and he had a very serious girlfriend—I'd always seen him through platonic eyes. Never noticing him as…a man…with really nice, green eyes.

I took off my glasses and pressed my fingers to my temples trying to massage away some of the tension. I couldn't start thinking that way.

He's my lifeline in this country where I don't have a very

good grasp of the language and the customs. Sure, I could find another person who speaks French, but it's not as if I could just pluck someone off the street tomorrow. It takes a special personality to relate to the public. Finding a replacement would mean down time for the tour, losing the momentum I've built and the money I've invested.

So unless I want to end up back at Pemberley, this is no time to get girlie over my business partner.

The front door to the office opened and closed. Without even seeing him, I knew it was Raoul meeting me here as we have most mornings of the past three weeks so that we could go collect our clients together. The office is right around the corner from the Hôtel du Carrousel. It made sense to meet here and arrive together—a unified team.

"*Bonjour!*" I called.

I straightened some papers and waited for him to appear at my office door.

"*Bonjour, Esme.*"

What I really didn't expect was the way my pulse kicked into high gear when our gazes met.

It was ridiculous.

Folding my hands in my lap, I drew in a calming deep breath and collected myself before I spoke.

"I'm glad you're here. I need to talk to you for a moment before we head out. Come in."

I gestured to a chair in front of my desk. As he sat down,

I ignored the vague thought of whether or not I'd put on lipstick. Oh, it didn't matter.

How could I have imagined him as Mr. Darcy? He wasn't Darcy-like at all. He was my friend. He was better suited as Johnny Depp's gypsy character in Chocolat—

"Is everything all right?" he asked.

"Yes. No. Umm—" My toes curled in my sensible low-heeled black pumps. "Listen, first, I want to apologize for my mother's behavior yesterday."

He laughed. "What are you talking about? She is charming."

I looked up at the ceiling and shook my head.

"I wouldn't call her charming. Mortifying, perhaps."

"Is she staying with you?" he asked.

"No. She asked, but I made it clear we'd both be better off if she stayed at the hotel. Besides, her room is already paid for." I leaned forward. "Look, I know you only covered for her because she asked you to help with her surprise. But I need you to promise me you won't egg her on while she's with us this week."

His brow furrowed. "Egg her on? *Pardon?*"

Uggg. This was making my head hurt. "Egg her on. You know, *don't* encourage her."

He tilted his head to the side. "*Non, je ne comprends pas*—err—I do not understand."

Despite how he indulged me those evenings he listened to me vent about her antics, there was no earthly way I could begin to make him understand my mother. I didn't even understand her.

Darcy.

Pemberley.

His lips on mine.

His hand on my body— Stop it!

"Raoul, she's a loose cannon, and we really need to make sure nothing goes wrong this week. Okay?"

He sat back and ran a hand over his jaw. "Why would it not be fine? Do you think your mother would come here to purposely sabotage our business?"

This was one of those great cultural divides I mentioned earlier—the type of thing that gets lost in translation that I depend on him to understand and translate for me. What was I supposed to do when my translator didn't understand?

"I just don't want anything to go wrong, okay?"

He got up from the chair and walked around behind me where he began massaging my shoulders. I relaxed into his touch.

"Esme, you need to—how do you say?—loosen up?"

His hands moved to my neck and I sank into the heavenly feel of it.

"Raoul—"

"*Shhh…* There is such a thing as killing the fun because you try to make something too perfect, no?"

No! I whirled around to look at him. "That's not what—"

"Yes." He nodded. "You show our clients you are having fun and they will have fun. *Voilà*. Even with your *mama*, 'twill be perfect."

Then he smiled like the devil.

"You do know how to have fun, Esme Valentine? Or must I teach you?"

As Raoul and I walked to the Hôtel du Carrousel from the office, the entire way I contemplated what he meant about teaching me how to have fun. Finally coming to the conclusion that I was reading meaning into his words because of that ridiculous dream.

That made sense, and I felt better.

The first person we saw when we entered the lobby was my mother.

The way the morning had started, it was a relief she'd decided to play nice and be on time. After I'd called her on the punctuality carpet yesterday, the rest of the day was a roller coaster—up one minute, down the next. Today her mood could've gone either way. Since she was the first of the clients to arrive, she was no doubt making a point. Fine with me. As long as her *point* didn't poke holes in the schedule, she could point away.

This was one of the busiest days of the tour since we were spending a considerable amount of time exploring the Louvre and the significant paintings mentioned in the book. We had two guest speakers and a full day of tours. It was imperative that we adhere to the schedule in order to fit everything in.

Of all days, today I didn't have time for any of her funny business. That's why it was disarming to find her perched in the lobby like a queen on her throne.

"*Bonjour,* y'all." She flashed her best smile and waved.

With that, I decided to meet her halfway and softened my stance.

Raoul kissed her hand and murmured, "*Bonjour, madame.* You look lovely this morning, Georgia."

My mother tittered.

Oh, please.

"Good morning, Mother. Thank you for being prompt. You do realize this morning everyone is having breakfast on their own. Did you eat?"

She waved away the suggestion as if it were unappetizing. "Heavens no. I can't stomach the thought of food until at least noon."

"Just as long as you realize we won't have time to stop until lunch."

She nodded. "But come to think of it, I would love a cup of coffee. I tried to get a cup to go, but I couldn't seem to make them understand what I wanted." She sighed. "They kept trying to give me coffee in a china cup. Of course, I had to pass. I certainly couldn't take a chance on being late and holding everyone up."

She pursed her red lips and looked me in the eye. "So here I am. No coffee for me. But I'm on time."

I ignored her and thumbed through my folder, looking for the day's itinerary. She would not rankle me. Nope. Not today.

"But you know, Raoul," she said, stretching out his name so it sounded like Raaaooooul, her voice inflecting on the "oooo." "You being a Frenchman and all, I'll bet you could sweet talk 'em into finding a paper cup. Come on, let's you and me hunt up a cup of joe to go."

She stood, adjusted her wraparound top so that just the right amount of cleavage peeked through and smiled, that old familiar twinkle in her eyes.

Oh, no.

Raoul shot me a wary glance, then looked back at her. "Actually, table service is standard in most cafés."

She batted her eyes. Yes. She actually batted. And she hit a home run.

"Oh, come on, Raoul. If ever there was a man who could scare up a little ol' paper cup, it's you. And I would be ever so grateful. In fact, you'd be my hero."

She dipped her chin and looked up at him through her feathery top lashes, smiling so that her dimples winked at him.

He shoved his hands in his pockets, succumbing to her wiles.

Exasperation pushed hard at my poker face as he shifted

his gaze to me, daring me to say no, to prove that indeed I did not know how to have fun.

I would have said no, but the elevator dinged, and a group of clients stepped into the lobby. Good sense slammed the cage door on *No!*, trapping it, thrashing and angry, inside. Somehow, I managed to swallow it.

I motioned Raoul over and whispered. "We leave in ten minutes. *Please* don't let her make you late."

He smiled.

I felt like the too-strict parent leveling a curfew. That was the story of my life. I'd always played the serious Lizzy Bennet to my mother's overly dramatic Mrs. Bennet. Except that Mrs. Bennet raised her daughters and didn't leave a succession of maddening Mr. Bennets for someone more fun. Come to think of it, maybe my mother was more like Lizzy's fickle younger sister Kitty—

I had to stop thinking in terms of *Pride and Prejudice*. And Pemberley. And Mr. Darcy...

He started to walk away, but I grabbed his arm.

"What is French for 'Run! Run far away from that woman'?"

He laughed. "*Sauve-toi. Fuis. Loin de cette femme.*"

I gave his arm a little squeeze, "Okay then, Raoul, *sauve-toi. Fuis. Loin de cette femme!*"

As I greeted the others, I watched my mother slip her arm through Raoul's as they walked out of the hotel into the sunny morning.

"THE MONA LISA IS SUCH a masterpiece because Leonardo da Vinci deemed her his finest accomplishment," said the first speaker in the day's series of lectures on the various paintings mentioned in the book. This lecture on the Mona Lisa, in the Louvre's great, crowded Denon Wing, was about the sacred feminine in art.

Raoul was up front. Mom stayed to the back of the group with me, muttering little asides.

"You must get so bored listening to the same *blah-blah-blah* over and over again. How can you stand it? I haven't even heard it the first time and—"

She made a gun with her thumb and index finger, held it to her temple and pretended to pull the trigger.

I frowned, embarrassed by her crass gesture. "Actually, it's pretty interesting if you give it a chance. I learn something new every time I hear the lecture."

"Yeah, I'll bet you could repeat the talk verbatim."

Despite the noisy crowds not affiliated with our tour milling through the gallery, the speaker paused and looked over at us. Embarrassed, I nudged my mother and pressed my index finger to my lips.

She rolled her eyes and sauntered over to a far wall of paintings that had nothing to do with the lecture. I wanted to ask her why she didn't try to listen. How could a person deem something boring before she even gave it a fair shake?

Given my mother's track record, I wondered if she

suffered from adult attention deficit disorder. Be it tours about famous novels, marriage or raising a daughter, she seemed to have a hard time staying with any one thing for an extended period of time.

My phone vibrated in my suit coat pocket. I fished it out and looked at the screen.

The office.

I hurried out of the gallery, trying to make it to a spot where I could answer the phone without disrupting the talk again.

"*Bonjour*, Solange," I said once I finally reached a place where I could answer. "*Ça va?*"

"*Bonjour*, Esme. *Ça va*. I am calling because the restaurant that you will visit for lunch today called…." She paused and I heard papers rustling in the background. I tensed, fearing a last-minute cancellation. *Surely not*. That would be a problem.

"Ah, here it is. They must change the menu."

I let out a breath. Change was fine. I could deal with change. Just not cancellations that would leave a big fat hole in the lunch plans.

"They cannot serve the spinach salad as you contracted, but will upgrade the salad course to the more expensive mixed baby greens with Roquefort and walnuts. No extra charge."

My stomach growled, and I placed a hand over it. "Not a problem, Solange. *Merci. Au revoir.*"

I hung up the phone and turned around to go back into

the gallery, nearly bumping into Mom, who stood not two feet behind me.

"Mother, you scared me. Why aren't you in there with the others?"

She shrugged.

I squinted at her, the first tinges of a headache knocking at my temples. "Mom, those lectures are one of the highlights of this tour. It's what you paid for. Go in there and get your money's worth."

I half-expected her to make a snide comment about how if I were a good daughter I'd refund her money. Because daughters don't make a profit off their mothers. Even though she signed up for it on her own accord, I did feel a little odd about making a profit off my mother. Perhaps I could have Solange figure how much I need to cover the expenses—hotel, food, admissions—and I could refund the rest— Oh, I'd think about it later.

"Actually, you know what would make me feel like I'd gotten my money's worth?"

I raised a brow and braced myself. "What?"

"If we could sit down just the two of us and…and…catch up. I know how busy you are, but…" Her words trailed off, but she raised her chin as if squaring off against an inner demon. "If you could just give me some time before the end of the week, that would make it all worth it to me."

Wow. That was unexpected. So not like her. To want

GET FREE BOOKS and FREE GIFTS
WHEN YOU PLAY THE...

SLOT MACHINE GAME!

Just scratch off the silver box with a coin. Then check below to see the gifts you get!

YES! I have scratched off the silver box. Please send me the 2 free Harlequin® Next™ books and 2 free gifts for which I qualify. I understand I am under no obligation to purchase any books, as explained on the back of this card.

355 HDL ELXX   155 HDL EL5M

FIRST NAME

LAST NAME

ADDRESS

APT.#

CITY

STATE/PROV.

ZIP/POSTAL CODE

7 7 7	**Worth TWO FREE BOOKS plus 2 BONUS Mystery Gifts!**
🍒 🍒 🍒	**Worth TWO FREE BOOKS!**
♣ ♣ ♣	**Worth ONE FREE BOOK!**
🔔 🔔 🍒	**TRY AGAIN!**

www.eHarlequin.com

(H-N-05/07)

Offer limited to one per household and not valid to current Harlequin® Next™ subscribers.

Your Privacy - Harlequin Books is committed to protecting your privacy. Our Privacy Policy is available online at www.eHarlequin.com or upon request from the Harlequin Reader Service. From time to time we make our lists of customers available to reputable firms who may have a product or service of interest to you. If you would prefer for us not to share your name and address, please check here ☐.

DETACH AND MAIL CARD TODAY!

© 2000 HARLEQUIN ENTERPRISES LTD.
® and ™ are trademarks owned and used by the trademark owner and/or its licensee.

The Harlequin Reader Service® — Here's how it works:

Accepting your 2 free books and 2 free mystery gifts places you under no obligation to buy anything. You may keep the books and gifts and return the shipping statement marked "cancel". If you do not cancel, about a month later we'll send you 4 additional books and bill you just $3.99 each in the U.S. or $4.74 each in Canada, plus 25¢ shipping & handling per book and applicable taxes if any.* That's the complete price and — compared to cover prices of $5.50 each in the U.S. and $6.50 each in Canada — it's quite a bargain! You may cancel at any time, but if you choose to continue, every other month we'll send you 4 more books, which you may either purchase at the discount price or return to us and cancel your subscription.

*Terms and prices subject to change without notice. Sales tax applicable in N.Y. Canadian residents will be charged applicable provincial taxes and GST. All orders subject to approval. Credit or debit balances in a customer's account(s) may be offset by any other outstanding balance owed by or to the customer. Please allow 4 to 6 weeks for delivery.

If offer card is missing write to: Harlequin Reader Service, 3010 Walden Ave., P.O. Box 1867, Buffalo NY 14240-1867

BUSINESS REPLY MAIL
FIRST-CLASS MAIL   PERMIT NO. 717   BUFFALO, NY

POSTAGE WILL BE PAID BY ADDRESSEE

HARLEQUIN READER SERVICE
3010 WALDEN AVE
PO BOX 1867
BUFFALO NY 14240-9952

NO POSTAGE
NECESSARY
IF MAILED
IN THE
UNITED STATES

to spend time with me? Not demanding, or conspiring or trying to manipulate me into doing what she wanted *right now, on her terms.*

Okay, what was she up to?

Still, something in her eyes made her look vulnerable, like a sail that had lost its wind.

I admit it, I was curious. It was rare that my mother and I settled down to talk face-to-face, usually we kept it to rushed superficial phone calls. I glanced at my watch. We had a little less than an hour before the lecture ended.

I held up a finger. "Wait here for a minute and I'll be right back."

She scanned the crowded area and I actually saw her radar zero in on a lone Asian man sitting on a bench with the space next to him free. I watched her saunter over and sit down next to him, her skirt hiking up a bit as she crossed her legs and leaned in to him.

"You. Speak. English?" she said.

He smiled and said, "I certainly do."

I couldn't watch anymore. Flirting was as intrinsic to her as breathing. There was no way she was giving up men. Not that she *should,* but there was something kind of comforting in the idea of my mother just being…my mother for a while— not the Mrs. Husband Number Six, a rebound marriage that was sure to go the way of all her other rebound marriages.

As I slipped back into the gallery to tell Raoul that I'd

be away for about a half hour, I couldn't help but wonder how our lives might have been different had my father lived? Realist that I am, the only conclusion I could come to was this was the hand I was dealt and I would live with it. Wasting energy wishing for what could never be was— well, just that, a waste of energy.

Returning, I said, "Come on, I want to show you something."

She looked askance at me, but followed without question. In fact, neither of us said a word as I led her from the Denon Wing over to the Sully area. No matter how many times I come to the Louvre, I always marvel at the sheer magnitude of the old palace and the art it houses.

Finally, we stopped in front of the stone lady herself, Venus de Milo.

"Well, look at that," Mom said. "There she is."

I nodded. "I thought you might like to see her."

We stood in silence for a moment, gazing up at her.

Finally Mom said, "She looks like she's been through hell. Missing two arms and she's still standing. I guess she's been through a lot worse than me, huh?"

My mother had tears in her eyes.

I was a little taken aback by this first glimpse of my mother's emotion.

"That's a good way to look at it. Did Benny leave you for someone else?"

Her gaze fixed on the Aphrodite, she nodded. "Younger. More vivacious. She's some hotshot pharmaceutical sales rep who called on his office all the time. He said it was just one of those things. I never thought he liked independent women. Always seemed like he needed someone who needed him. I guess the joke's on me."

Her words rolled out in a nervous tumble.

Then she was quiet again. Glancing around. Wringing her hands and looking a little uncomfortable.

After a long, silent pause, she said, "Maybe I should've paid more attention to things like those lectures you're so crazy about. Had my own life like you do. Maybe he would've loved me more if I'd been smarter about classy things like that."

She chuckled, but it tapered off to a sigh.

"Maybe I should've been more like you. Not afraid to be alone."

When I was growing up, she reminded me of a butterfly— undeniably beautiful, effortlessly inspiring men to run after her and always hard to pin down. I was forever chasing after her, and she was just out of my reach. If I did manage to catch her, she'd flit and flutter, desperate to escape.

I was that trace of cocoon that stuck to her back; an irritant of which she was desperate to free herself.

But today, the way the light slanted across her face, casting shadows, she looked old and tired. The luminosity that had always lit her from within had been snuffed out.

As hard as it was to admit, this new, *flat* version of my mother, the one who had sworn off men, made the world seem a little off kilter.

The loop playing in my head said, *Be careful what you wish for*. Because for years, I'd wished for this more subdued version of my mother and now that I had her, I didn't know what to do with her.

"I don't know about that, Mom. I'm me and you're you. Obviously, my independence hasn't garnered me any long-lasting relationships."

She turned in a slow circle, taking in the other statues in their nude bronze and marble glory.

"I probably should've never married him in the first place. Oh, dear God, when did I become a walking cliché? When did I get old?"

A tear meandered down her cheek, and her hand shook as she brushed it away. I reached out and touched her fingers, feeling a little unnerved by this foreign intimacy and subdued side of my mother.

She flinched, pulling away from me. Her chest rose and fell with the weight of her emotion.

I should've been a bigger person, should've been stronger, but her pulling away from me hurt much more than I thought possible. She could be so open with others, give away so much of herself to people she ended up throwing away, but with me, she was so closed.

The great wall that had always stood between us was still intact.

"Paris is so lovely," she said not looking at me. "You know, I was serious yesterday when I said I wanted to live here. And, well, I don't know of an easy way to ask you this, so I'm just going to blurt it out and not beat around the bush." She cleared her throat. "Esme, I was wondering if I could live with you here until I get settled in my own place? I know it's a lot to spring on you. So you don't have to answer me now." She chewed on her bottom lip. Her eyes darting from me to the artwork and back to me. "In fact, please don't answer me now. Think about it and we'll talk when you're ready."

10:30 p.m.

On the third day of the tour we took a daytrip to the countryside about an hour outside of Paris to Château Villette, the fictional home of a character in the book.

The grand seventeenth-century estate sits on one hundred eighty-five acres. Still, I could've used more space to avoid my mother and her anxious looks that projected, *So what'll it be? Will you take me in?*

She didn't come right out and ask, of course. Which was a good thing. Because, no, I hadn't made up my mind. How in the world was I supposed to do this? It was a recipe for disaster.

After we dropped the guests off at the hotel, I was too wound up to go home. So I went to the office to check on the progress of future tours, check e-mail, organize the next day and seek counsel from my friend Marie.

"Yes, I'm serious." I cradled the phone between my ear and my shoulder as I logged onto my computer. "The woman who's wanted very little to do with me for most of my life asked if she could move in with me."

I checked my e-mail as I listened to Marie's stunned silence. Finally, she found her words.

"What is she going to do while she's here? Does she realize for an American to live in France, she must cut through reams of governmental red tape and jump through an obstacle course of bureaucratic hoops before she can secure her visa?"

Nobody knew this better than me. It took years of planning and going back and forth between London and Paris before I could legally move here and set up shop. I finally took the plunge six months ago and moved here to start the French arm of Valentine Tours.

"She can't even speak the language," Marie said.

"Neither can I."

"Yes, but at least you're taking classes."

"The language my mother is most fluent in is pretty universal and doesn't have many words— Oh, that reminds me. Did I tell you what happened in my class last week?"

"No."

"The instructor, Emily, is this très chic, 'mature' French woman, who has to be in her late sixties at the very least. She's very intelligent—speaks fluent Spanish, Italian and English in addition to French, of course—but she vaguely reminds me of that seventies-era Saturday Night Live Gilda

Radner character Emily Litella. Do you know who I mean? That older lady who confuses similar words and ends up saying—'Oh! That's different. Never mind.'"

"*Non*, I don't believe I know that character."

"Well, I don't know why she makes me think of her. Perhaps it's because her name is Emily, or maybe it's because she's very absentminded.

"At any rate, last class only seven women show up (three of them were named Mary). We got a little rowdy while reviewing our verbs. Emily sidetracked into how she's married to a German who refused to learn French. She said she once gave her husband the silent treatment for six days because she was mad at him for not studying his French verbs.

"Someone asked, 'How can you speak if you don't have a common language?'

"Mary number one said, 'Obviously, they don't need words to communicate. Oooh la la. It's so French.'

"Mary number two joked that he'd be getting no *action* if he didn't learn his verbs.

"Then the rowdiest Mary said, 'Emily, did you marry your husband for his body?'

"Emily loved this. She said, 'His body *est magnifique*. He's thirty years younger than I. Alas, I married him because *j'adore* him.'

"Seven jaws hit the floor."

"*Non*," says Marie.

"I'm not kidding. But I wondered if it was a marriage of convenience for a visa?"

"Oh, why must you always be so cynical when it comes to matters of the heart, Esme? Maybe they're in love."

"Oh my God, Marie, you have to admit there's a definite freaky-factor there."

I wanted to say to Marie that the cynic in me kept waiting for Emily to say, "Oh, you thought I said thirty years? No, I said dirty ears… That's different. Never mind." But I wasn't sure the joke would translate.

"*Non*, I choose to think *MERDE!* You go, girl! There's hope for us after all! I mean why should we think we are less appealing to men because we age? I think that is a definite French/American difference in thinking."

I leaned back in my chair, stretching my tired legs out in front of me, considering what she said. "Yeah, that's a nice thought. If I ever had time to meet someone who was staying in Paris longer than a week."

"You must make time to have fun, Esme."

What was that? The theme of the week? I knew how to have fun, I'd just been in work mode for so long, it was hard to switch gears. If things kept going as well as they had been, in another month I might be able to take a little time off. Although, even the thought scared me a little. What in the world would I do with myself?

The door in the outer office opened and closed and I tensed until Raoul appeared in the threshold of my office.

"I have to go," I said to Marie. "Raoul's here."

"One last thought before I hang up. Maybe this is the opportunity for you and your mother to have a relationship? I know it's crazy, but please don't close your mind.

"Have fun with Raoul. Now, there's a fine man who's in town for more than a week." Her laugh sounded like a cat's purr. "*Bonsoir*, Esme."

Oh for God's sake. "Goodbye, Marie."

As I hung up, heat spread over my face like wildfire and the Pemberley dream flashed in my head. I was glad the only light in the room was the small desk lamp.

"Raoul, what are you doing here so late?"

His gaze lingered on mine. "I could ask you the same question. I came by to leave this for you." He held up a CD and a red piece of paper. "I didn't want to call you at home because I thought it might be too late, but obviously I would not have succeeded in finding you at home."

"What's that?"

He walked in and settled in one of the chairs across from my desk propping his right ankle on his left knee.

"I have good news and I have bad news. Which would you like to hear first?"

I closed my laptop so I could see him better. "Give me the good news first, because I've had plenty of challenges for one day."

He nodded. "*Regardez—errr*… Look. At this." He took a piece of folded paper from his jacket pocket and held it out across my desk.

I looked down at the advertisement, able to make out the key words: *Le Chat Rouge*—a club; Montmartre—the location; *Le Django Gypsies*, which I assumed was the name of a band that was playing at *Le Chat Rouge*.

I glanced back up at him, unnerved by the intensity of his gaze, steadfastly watching me as I perused the flyer. "This is the good news?"

Raoul nodded as he stood and walked over to an armoire that housed tour brochures and a stereo system I rarely used. He popped in the CD.

I pushed the red paper to the side of my desk as a jaunty tune featuring violin, acoustic guitar and an underlying thump of bass came through the speakers. It sounded tinny, like something from the 1930s—like jazz with a hint of bluegrass. What I imagined to be brasserie music. The type of tune that inspires one to tap her foot and snap her fingers in time with the beat—if she were so inclined. But I wasn't, despite the way Raoul beamed at me, his green eyes sparkling. "You like?"

From the speakers emerged a voice edged with a slightly nasal French accent singing in English. I listened to a few more bars and shrugged. "Yes… It's…different. It's nice. I suppose."

He shot me an incredulous look. "Nice? *Non,* it's more

than *nice*. It is my brother, Jean, and his *quintette*. They are in Paris for a special engagement on this month of the Django Reinhardt celebration. You know the artist Django Reinhardt?"

I nodded, vaguely familiar with the music of the French gypsy jazz guitarist.

Raoul puffed out his chest. "What's more is Django, he was a distant cousin of Jean and myself."

"This is the good news?" I repeated, unsure of where he was going with this.

"Yes, we must take the tour to Montmartre to hear *Le Django Gypsies* Thursday evening."

He crosses his arms over his chest.

"Nice thought." I slid the flyer across the desk. "We've booked the tour into a show."

He shrugged in that French manner I found incredibly endearing. "Which brings me to the bad news. It seems that the actors in the show have organized a strike and will not perform until a compromise is reached."

A strike. One of the most maddening aspects of French life. On any given day one organization or another—be it metro drivers or museum workers or you name it—someone was angry and going on strike.

He held up a finger. "Ah, but it will be fun. A little music. A little dancing at this special Django Reinhardt celebration. They will love it."

I cocked my head to the side listening to the boisterous violin and guitar combo. "This has nothing to do with the book. At least the show was vaguely related from the art angle." The way he looked at me seemed to say, *Help me out. What other options do we have?*

"Your brother, huh?"

He nodded vigorously. "Playing in the style of my distant cousin." A smile of pride spreads across his face. My God he was handsome….

"No offence to *your* brother or distant cousin, but how in the world do you think people can dance to this? I mean, it's fun, but it's not danceable. We'd better bill it as a special festival."

He puckered his lips. "*Au contraire*, Esme. It could be a very romantic night of dancing."

I blew out a soft *prove-it pfffft*.

He arched a brow and crossed back to the armoire and punched a button. A slower song filled the air. Slower in comparison to the earlier tune that might have been suitable for square dancing. Well, perhaps that was a slight exaggeration… Still, this one had a four-four rhythm that reminded me of how we used to count out quarter notes in my elementary school music class. One, two, three, four. A familiar tune, but I couldn't quite place it.

"You must use your imagination." Raoul offered me his hand.

"What? No. No! I don't dance—"

He pulled me to my feet with one quick tug, walked me around to the front of my desk.

"Let me show you. Just follow me and you will see it is easy and very—how you say—danceable?"

By the time we got into waltz position, I recognized the song as *I Can't Give You Anything But Love*, which was…nice and, okay, even a little romantic. A ripple of awareness coursed through me—the feel of his shoulder under my hand…the feel of his hand on my back…the other one holding my hand… I shook away the thought and focused on how even though I knew nothing about formal dancing, I knew we couldn't waltz to this song because a waltz required a three-four rhythm and this was definitely four-four…

But the next thing I knew Raoul and I were moving around the room in a slow, sensual—and yes, slightly awkward—dance. I suppose I was a little flustered because I couldn't remember the last time I'd danced with a man…like this…being so close to him… He smelled good and that sent a shiver skittering down my body. No. It wasn't the nearness of him that flustered me so.

It had to be the whole ridiculousness of it—the way we kept stepping on each other and bumping into each other. I mean, come on, dancing in my office?

"Raoul—"

"*Shhh*…just relax." He tugged my left hand. But my hand

barely moved. He frowned. "You are too tense. You try to lead when you do not know what you are doing. Why must you always lead?"

I jerked away, breathing a little easier after regaining my personal space. "Excuse me? I *do* know what I'm doing." *No you don't. You are so far out of your league.* "And I don't *always* have to lead."

He raised his hands. "You told me you do not know how to dance, *n'est pas?* I can teach you if you will stop trying to lead."

He pulled me back into his arms.

I didn't always have to lead....

I could be a lady.

I consciously relaxed my shoulders, which only seemed to push the tension into my arms and hands. So I loosened my grip on his hands, flexing my fingers a little. He pushed the slightest bit on my hand guiding me as he lifted his foot to step forward.

I stepped back.

"*Oui*, that's right," he murmured, smiling down at me.

Our dance wasn't smooth. Oh, he was fine. I was the one who was all clumsy left feet, which made me tense up all over again.

"Relax," he murmured, shifting closer.

I allow myself to drift into the moment, savoring the smell of him, the feel of him...pretty soon we fell into a rhythm.

"I think I might actually be getting the hang of this."

"Shhh...." Raoul pulled me closer. Our bodies moved together as the singer crooned about not being able to give anything but love and having plenty of it....

He shifted again so that our bodies were flat against each other. His hand caressed my back...his breath hot on my temple...his lips skimmed my cheekbone... I looked up at him and his eyes were hazy and hooded and the next thing I knew his lips were on mine.

I can't tell you how long we stood like that, holding each other, kissing each other. My common sense screamed for me to stop, but another part, a deeper, hungry part wanted to disappear into the shelter of his arms, into a place where everything tuned out like it did at the end of a Jane Austen novel—nice and neat, everyone with their soul mate.

Still, as the kiss ended, the realist in me knew that real life was a far cry from a novel. I mean, let's face it, in real life the Goddess of Love didn't always smile down upon you. She certainly hadn't favored my mother and me.

It may not have mattered to my mother. She kept jumping from one relationship right into the next because she couldn't stand to be alone.

I, on the other hand, was not quite as resilient as my mother. Losing my father, and essentially my mother (for most of my life), Kyle and my grandmother proved that all of the major relationships in my life went south before I was ready to let go.

I did not want to test the fates with Raoul.

So that's why when he slowly pulled back and said, "I've wanted to do that for a very long time."

All I could do was walk to my desk and say with my back to him, "I think *Le Chat Rouge* will work well as a substitute for the Thursday night outing."

8:30 *a.m.*

Pretending as if nothing had changed between us, Raoul and I carried on business as usual. We marched the group down the rue Bonaparte, to Place Saint-Sulpice, where we stopped to regroup while admiring the square. A friend once described the area as "a piece of heaven in the heart of a busy city."

Of course, this quieter, greener, more tranquil piece of heaven came with a hefty price tag, the houses in this area are among the most expensive in Paris. Looking around, you could imagine why. People loved to live here between the gently spouting nineteenth-century fountains; they loved to lounge on benches beneath ancient chestnut trees. Above the square, the towers of Saint-Sulpice rose high above the neighboring roofs. It was another world, this serene beauty, but even its peaceful tranquility couldn't stop me from thinking of Raoul's kiss and how it would change the dynamics of things.

So rather than deal with it, I dove headlong into work, explaining to the clients how the first stone of the existing church facade was laid in 1646 around the remains of an older and smaller church.

Still, most of my lecture took a back seat to what the clients came to see—thanks to all the hype surrounding "The Book." They wanted to glimpse the simple copper line that runs through the middle of the choir, the zero meridian of Paris.

So while Raoul was beginning his talk about the meridian line and the group was gazing at the floor, I realized I had two choices (and I had to decide fast): I could pretend as if nothing happened in my office last night or I could flat out tell him what happened would never happen again.

He'd understand. In fact, maybe he'd be relieved that I didn't go all clingy on him. After all, flirting is a recreational sport among Frenchmen. World-class *footsie* is the national sport—second only to World Cup *football*.

My mother stood next to me.

"Have you had a chance to think any more about me moving in with you?"

"Good morning, Mother. I'm fine and you?"

Looking contrite, she pulled her bottom lip between her teeth. "I'm sorry. I guess I'm just anxious to figure out what I'm going to do."

I felt like a heel for being such a grouch. I took a deep breath and softened my stance.

"I'm still thinking about it."

She nodded.

"Before I decide, I need to ask you two questions."

Her eyes widened as if she was expecting the inquisition.

"Why Paris and why do you want to move in with me?"

She looked pensive, as if weighing her words before an important oral exam.

I wasn't trying to bring her to her knees. All I wanted was to hear her say *I need you....*

She wrung her hands. "I just thought that..." The butterfly was fluttering, afraid of being pinned down, ready to fly away.

"I mean... You're so good at standing on your own two feet. So self-sufficient, I thought..."

Her words trailed off and she stood there for a moment looking panicked. Then she smiled and her big, hazel eyes got even larger. "Oh, baby, Benny's leaving made me realize I let things get in the way."

I crossed my arms, a defense against my disappointment that the conversation had turned back to Benny. "Well then you need to go back to Florida and talk things out with him at home. Moving to Paris will just be one more thing that'll get in the way."

She knit her brow, confused.

"I don't think you understand. I've let men come between *us*. You and me, Esmeralda."

It took a moment for the words to sink in. Just as they were, she elbowed me and said, "But you have to admit with as successful as you are, I must not have been a complete failure as a mother."

I stared at her in disbelief. How could she even suggest that she deserved a smidgeon of the credit for how my life turned out?

She crossed her arms, mirroring me. "Oh, don't look at me that way. I'm joking. I take absolutely no credit for how wonderful you've turned out. That was your grandma's doing. Her doing and the fact that you always were an independent little cuss. But you know, baby, I always respected that in you."

We were quiet for a moment, Raoul's tour speech echoing in the background.

"But, Mom, how could you leave your own daughter. Do you know it always felt like you chose them over me."

At least she had the grace to bow her head. "I tried, Esme. I really tried. But it got to the point where I could see that it was unfair to you to keep yanking you in and out of schools, moving you here and there. You had a much better life with your grandmother. She loved you so much. She gave you a better home than I ever could have. Plus, I thought that by letting you stay with her, you'd somehow have a little piece of your father."

I couldn't speak. I couldn't even look at her. I just stood there feeling like stone.

"I've always been so proud of you, Esme. But I guess I've always been afraid of you, too. Afraid that if I got too close, I'd infect you with my screwed up ways."

I wanted to say, *So that's your excuse for not even trying? You burst onto the scene after all these years and make me want to let you into my life so you'll leave again? I'm doing fine without you. Just like I have all these years.*

"Well, I just thought..."

"Why, Mom, after all these years have you decided it's time to get close?"

She looked deflated. "Do I need a reason? If I said I'm sorry for all the wasted years would it help? Because I am sorry. Terribly sorry."

I was weighing my words—

"Why is everyone staring at the floor?" she asked.

Her non sequitur threw me, but I followed her gaze to Raoul and the group.

"They're looking at the rose line," I said.

She tilted her head to the side. "The rose line?"

"It's the meridian." I pointed out. "That brass line in the floor— Mom, have you even read the book that this tour's based on?"

A look passed over her that suggested the idea had never occurred to her.

Of course not.

Then the expression was gone as quickly as it appeared and we both quietly listened to Raoul.

"Mmm-mmm." My mother shook her head and bit her bottom lip. "I just find something irresistible about a smart man with an accent."

I slanted a glance at her. "Men with brains. Do they rank higher or lower than the intellectually challenged and the marginally intelligent men you've loved so well?"

She rolled her eyes. "That's not very nice, Esmeralda."

Feeling more like myself, I squared my shoulders.

"Mom, face it, you're an equal opportunity lover. With your...err...*appreciation* of men, I can't take you seriously when you claim you've sworn off men forever and ever amen."

She looked completely taken aback. "Well, I didn't say it was for the rest of my life."

I did my best to resist pulling an *I-told-you-so* face. "Usually when one makes a strong statement such as 'I'm finished with men,' *for the rest of my life* is implied.

"I knew you couldn't do it. That's why you need to go back to Florida when this trip is finished and face your problems, rather than moving here and running away from them."

She frowned.

"Someone got up on the wrong side of the bed today."

Reflexively, my gaze flickered back to Raoul.

"Oh, for heaven's sake, Esme. Just sleep with him already."

"What?" I wanted to scream. I wanted to tell her that I did not use men to fill what was missing in me. But Pat and Alice, her new friends, were motioning her to join the group as they spent the last few minutes on their own exploring Saint-Sulpice.

As I watched her laughing with the other women, a little voice inside me demanded, *If not a man then what? What will make me happy?* I'd obviously not found what I was searching for in London. So I'd come to Paris…still searching. Was that really any different from what my mother was doing?

Raoul walked over. For a few beats we stood in awkward silence watching the group mill about like parents observing a playgroup.

"Ça va, Esme?"

I studied his eyes, the strong line of his jaw, the curve of his upper lip, remembering how he tasted—a mixture of mint, coffee and man—craving another taste. I battled with myself over how to answer.

"I don't know. My mother is driving me crazy."

He nodded. "At least you are talking. It could be the first step toward healing."

He gave my arm a little squeeze.

Something inside me shifted, and it felt as if the concrete coating around my heart started to crumble.

"Raoul," my mother called to him from across the chapel. All three ladies motioned for him to come over. "Hon, come over here and explain this painting to us. You're just so good with all this art stuff. I do believe you could even talk me into being interested in it."

"Your fan club beckons."

Raoul looked at me and something new passed between us.

"How do you say—hold that thought." He smiled. "Duty calls. I must tend to our clients."

7:45 a.m.

"What do you mean you're quitting?" I asked in utter horror as I stood clutching the edge of my desk. "You can't just leave without notice. I'll need time to find someone to take your place."

Solange looked down her aquiline nose at me. "I certainly am quitting." She flipped her long, auburn hair over her slim shoulder. "I have another job and my new employer expects me today. I bid you *adieu*, Madame Valentine."

Madame Valentine? I didn't know which burned more—the lurch in which she was leaving me or the fact that she'd *madamed* me.

Maybe I was just sensitive since tomorrow was my birthday, and I'd done my best not to think about it. But at times like this, I desperately wished the French had a middle-ground courtesy title for those *of a certain age* who were still single and ignoring middle age—the equivalent of the English Ms.—anything other than *madame*.

It made me feel ancient. And really, thirty-five wasn't *that* old. Only when I let myself dwell on it for too long, did I start to feel old…and alone.

Which is why I spent so much time and energy on the business. It was an investment that paid off. What I put into it, it gave back and it never cheated or lied or took me for a fool….

Solange shut the front door, and I walked out into the tiny reception area, glancing around, lost.

Great. What would we do now?

She'd done more than merely answer the phone. If that's all she'd done, I could've used an answering machine—

An answering machine. Yes. Not ideal, but for the time being, at least it would receive the calls.

I sat at the reception desk and after a bit of trial and error, I succeeded in changing the after-hours message to a perky *your-business-is-important-to-us-leave-your-name-and-number-and-we'll-call-you-back* greeting.

Raoul arrived as I was playing it back. Despite the inconvenience of Solange leaving, it was almost a relief to have something to take the focus off this new personal situation blooming with Raoul.

He was just as surprised as I was at her quitting.

"I had no clue that she was unhappy here," I said, as we walked to the hotel to meet the guests. "Did she give you any indication she wasn't happy?"

"Unhappy? Why do you assume she was unhappy? Perhaps she simply received a better offer."

I stopped just short of the hotel doors and looked at him. He stopped, too.

"Then why didn't she give me a chance to match the offer. She's been here nearly six months, we could have given her a raise."

He shrugged. "We shall find someone else. She was not—how you say—irreplaceable."

I threw my hands into the air. "Raoul, how can you take this so lightly? There's so much to do—so much that's still not done. I need—"

He took a step toward me and cupped my chin in his hand, which completely threw off my train of thought.

"You worry too much, Esme Valentine. We will be fine. I know exactly what you need…."

The next thing I knew his lips were on mine and he was kissing me.

Again.

Right there.

In broad daylight.

I wouldn't go to dinner with him last night, but today I was kissing him back, fisting my hands into the cotton of his shirt, leaning into him as if my next breath depended on him.

There we were, on the sidewalk of that busy Paris street. At that particular moment, I couldn't remember its name.

And I didn't care.

Because it was a kiss that affected me all the way down to my curled toes inside my sensible low-heeled black pumps. Places inside me that had stirred the other night when we kissed in the office awoke fully this time, igniting and blossoming into a blaze.

He kissed me so thoroughly that I forgot my perfectly logical rationale for not mixing business with pleasure. Or maybe I no longer cared. The reasons began to shift and mist around the edges, until they transported me beyond Pemberley.

Because this was even better. This wasn't Mr. Darcy kissing Elizabeth Bennet. This was Raoul, holding me close, kissing my lips, making any other *romantic fantasies* seem pretty much irrelevant.

"You are right," he said, his forehead against mine, his lips barely a whisper away. "There is so much we have left undone. What are we going to do about that?"

His question mark was one last tiny kiss he planted on my lips.

I was so stunned. Or maybe stunned wasn't the right word. Maybe it was more apt to say he'd kissed me so thoroughly that I was speechless, questioning nothing, but at the same time, questioning all the personal rules I'd ever applied to my life.

I hadn't realized just how far outside the lines I'd been scribbling, until I heard the catcalls and applause.

We turned around and there was my mother and a handful of the tour clients standing outside the hotel entrance.

IT'S AMAZING HOW QUICKLY I recovered from the mortification I felt about that moment of indiscretion. I braced myself for an inquisition from my mother, but all she said was, "You go girl, at least one of us is getting some."

Maybe that was embarrassing enough, but the day's events soon picked up a pace of their own and we were all caught up in our picnic at the Bois de Boulogne. In *the book* the protagonists take a wild ride through the park at night. Like Dr. Jekyll and Mr. Hyde, the Bois is a beautiful place to visit during the day, but notoriously unsavory after sunset. For safety reasons, we opted for a daytime visit. Since we were in the vicinity, a tour and a few hours of on-their-own shopping in the posh Passy neighborhood rounded out the afternoon.

Since he wasn't a shopper, Raoul decided to go back to the office after lunch to place a help wanted ad in the newspaper. I hoped my mother would fall in with Pat and Alice so I could shop for a new outfit for tomorrow night's club visit. I justified it as an early birthday present to myself.

Still, my mother waved goodbye to Pat and Alice, determined that we would have a little mother-daughter time.

"Let's go get a cup of coffee," she said. "My treat."

We ended up at a little café not too far from the Trocadéro. Her face brightened. "Look at this adorable little place.

You're such a doll to do this now. One little *cupa* in the morning isn't doing it for me, baby. I needed a little something more to wake up these old bones."

We made small talk about the weather, the tour, Paris in general and Solange quitting and leaving Valentine Tours in a lurch. Then the server brought our *café crèmes*.

Mom dumped three packets of sugar in hers. Her spoon made a rhythmic *clink-clink-clink* as she stirred.

"So you're hiring?" she said.

I nodded as I took a too-hot sip of my coffee. It burned my tongue.

"So hire me."

I flinched, mad at myself for not seeing this coming.

"Mom, you need a visa before you can work here."

She shook her head. "I did some asking around at the hotel—such nice people, very helpful—well, except when it comes to coffee-to-go. They told me I could be here three months before I had to worry about a visa. What if I worked for you in exchange for room and board?"

I squeezed my eyes shut. "Mom, just…please. I don't know. I'd have to talk to Raoul before I could even consider it. Can we just drink our coffee in peace? Just enjoy each other without there being some sort of negotiation on the table?"

She looked a little hurt and I felt bad about it, but I *couldn't* give her an answer. I needed time to think it through.

We sat in silence for a few minutes. Until, finally, she

said, "Why didn't you want to tell me you and Raoul were involved?"

Heat flashed in my cheeks and I looked down into my cup as if I'd find the answer there.

Don't get defensive. She's trying to meet on middle ground.

"Mom, it's new. I don't even know if you'd call it *involved*. It's complicated, and I don't want to screw it up."

A sly smile overtook her face. She leaned in conspiratorially. "He cares for you, doll baby. If you'd just let him, it could be a very good thing."

I wanted to say, *You don't know that, Mom. Every fresh bloom of love seems like a good thing to you.*

"You know he talks to me about you."

Her words made my stomach clench.

"What do you mean?" I asked.

"What? Do you think he's been hanging around me because he's interested in this old gal?"

She laughed, but it was a little dry and regretful.

"Why not?" I asked.

She tried to wave away the question.

"Seriously, Mom, why not? Why wouldn't he be interested in you?"

She lifted a finger. "Wait a minute, maybe we should back up here and set the record straight. Even if he was interested in me I don't think I could go there. He could be my son."

"There's nothing wrong with a younger lover...especially when your libido is still as...umm...young as yours."

We both laughed.

"I didn't say there was anything wrong with taking a younger lover, it's just that...oh, I don't know, Esme. I'm tired these days. I'm tired of always chasing after that silver lining."

Her gaze grew distant.

"I've always believed in love," she said. "You know why?"

I shook my head.

"Because I had such a good relationship with your daddy. He was a good man, Esmeralda. And I suppose I was looking for him in all those men after him."

She paused for a moment to sip her coffee. Her words settled on my heart and all of a sudden things started to make sense. All the men over all the years after my father died...jumping from one to the next, not because she was bored, but because she was looking for *him*. She's known true love once and she was just looking for what she had with him.

She set down her cup. "It's taken me a long time, but I've come to the conclusion that maybe certain people only get one true love in a lifetime—"

It was perverse, but there was something a little unnerving about this notion coming from her. It felt like the Hershey Company ceasing production of chocolate because they'd determined it wasn't good for you.

Chocolate in small doses. Where would we be without

at least a little chocolate? Maybe even a little chocolate every day?

"Mom, you can't just give up. You're only fifty-three years old. Too young to swear off men."

All of a sudden it was as if something physically jolted her. She gazed back at me. "I don't know where you've gotten the notion that I'm swearing off men forever. I'm just taking a little break. A little break to stand on my own two feet. To learn to love *me*."

She was serious.

Any doubts I had about her motives evaporated right there in that Passy café.

"You can move in with me for a while, Mom. But I still have to talk to Raoul about the job. He has to be part of that decision."

Though we both knew he would likely agree.

She clapped her hands and squealed. People at the surrounding tables shot curious glances at us. My first reaction was to tell her *shhhh!* Everyone's looking at us.

But then that was replaced with a horror vision of what life with my mother would be like—her sleeping on the Hide-A-Bed sofa in the living room of my one-bedroom apartment. Her scarves and heels and bangles and baubles slowly taking over. Oh dear God, what had I done?

"I hope you don't mind sleeping on a sofa bed."

She shook her head.

"In the living room, because I'm not giving up my bedroom."

She raised her chin in that stubborn way of hers. "I wouldn't take your room if you offered it to me. I happen to love sofa beds. Some of the best sex of my life has happened on a pull-out couch."

"Mother! Too much information."

She smiled and put her hand on mine. For a few moments we both sat there like that, saying nothing, trying on this new trust.

Finally, she broke the silence. "I predict you'll end up spending a lot of nights over at Raoul's, anyway."

I resisted the urge to squirm. I stared at my mother's hand on mine and considered the possibility. Sitting right there at that Passy café, I decided to give myself another birthday present in addition to the outfit I'd planned to get for the *Le Chat Rouge* outing.

I'd give myself the gift of possibility. For once in my life, I'd scribble outside the lines and see where it got me. Because thus far, being so neat and tidy wasn't making me nearly as happy as I thought it would.

We finished our coffee.

She bought me a killer outfit. My birthday present, though she kept calling it my *birthday suit*, which did make me cringe. "Mom, shhhh!"

Ahh, but it was fabulous. A slinky little red dress that was so not me. It was more my mother's style—no surprise since she picked it out. It looked great and made me feel sexy. As I gazed at myself in the boutique mirror, I realized the person staring back represented everything I wished I could be, but could never admit until now.

Mom and I shared a cab back to the hotel. She wanted me to come up to the room because she had the perfect shoes and earrings to go with the dress.

We were laughing and making plans for tomorrow night. Then suddenly, Mom stopped in the middle of the lobby looking as if she'd seen a ghost.

"Benny, what on earth are you doing here?"

8:00 p.m.

Did I mention I usually don't enjoy celebrating my birthday? It's usually just another day.

Which is exactly what it turned out to be.

On this second to the last day of the tour, we had a trip to Versailles planned. My mother was a no-show.

I'm not going to whine about her not coming though, because I'm not mad at her. Not surprised. And if I were mad at anyone, it would be myself for getting my hopes up that she could really change.

When we saw Benny in the lobby, I had an inkling she'd go home with him. I had a feeling that as she turned and told me, "I'm sorry, honey, will you give me a rain check on accessorizing your dress? I need to deal with him alone."

This morning when I arrived at the hotel to meet the guests, she wasn't there. She'd given Pat a birthday card to give to me. Inside was a simple message: Happy Birthday!

Sorry I have to skip out today, lots to take care of. You wear that dress tonight and arrive in style. See you soon, Mom.

Not even Love, Mom.

Just the old familiar, *See you soon*.

My threadbare heart sank to the floor and for about fifteen seconds, I sank into my unhappiness, quietly absorbing what this meant.

Last time *soon* stretched into five years. But I suppose some could argue that I was partially to blame since planes do fly both ways over the Atlantic.

Whatever.

She'll go back to Benny—and maybe that's not such a bad thing, and I'll go back to my old *ocean between us* state of mind.

It hurts a lot less that way. Really, I'm okay with it.

So, I regrouped, and Raoul was sweet, bringing me a single red rose and a birthday pastry. He led the group in a frightful round of *Happy Birthday*, which made me want to crawl under the seat and hide, but I suppose it was the thought that counted.

So that was it for my birthday.

I was thirty-five, which didn't feel a bit different than thirty-four. Next year thirty-five would merge into thirty-six and so on and so on….

Just another day in the life….

Versailles was lovely. Everyone had a great time. Even if I did spend most of the day feeling a little lost. Feeling sort of like a tourist on my own tour.

During the bus ride back, I came this close to asking Raoul if he'd mind if I bowed out of the dinner at *Le Chat Rouge*. After all, it was my birthday. But the thought of spending the night alone, feeling sorry for myself seemed even less appealing.

When I got home, I put on the *Django Gypsies* CD, determined to change my mood. I contemplated *not* wearing the red "birthday suit." I even put on my typical boring uniform of black slacks and black sleeveless pullover, but it made me feel…just that—*très* boring.

So, five minutes before Raoul was set to pick me up—because earlier that day, he demanded, "The birthday girl would not venture out alone on her special night"—I did a presto-chango and donned that damn red dress. I don't know if it was to spite my mother or myself since I had to dig the only pair of black strappy sandals I own out of the back of my closet. I prayed I'd remember how to walk in them because it had been years since I'd last worn them.

I finally decided walking in heels is one of those things that's ingrained in us—like riding a bike or making love. Once you do it, you don't forget how, you just don't recall how good it can make you feel until you do it again.

The look on Raoul's face was worth it. When I opened the door, his jaw dropped. Really, I mean it. That in itself elevated my mood several levels.

Especially when he kissed me and murmured, "It is a

good thing our group is expecting us because the way you look tonight, I would probably keep you in and—"

"All rightie then. Let's get going."

Part of me felt shaky when it came to Raoul. Judging by the way he kissed me, he obviously seemed okay with the rate at which our relationship was progressing.

I didn't know. I just didn't know. Because just as I'd gone running for cover in my "ocean between us" mother philosophy, I wanted the familiar safety of compartmentalizing my business and personal lives, which I suppose would've amounted to shelving my personal life since Raoul was it in that category.

As we arrived at the hotel, the day was calling it a night. The sun hung low and grand, painting the wide western sky dramatic shades of pink, orange and violet.

I guess I didn't realize I'd been harboring one last tiny ember of hope that she'd be there.

But I was.

And she wasn't.

For the smallest millisecond, I was ten years old again, abandoned by my mother.

I DIDN'T CRY.

Because I'd learned at a young age it did no good. Served no purpose other than making your nose run.

When I felt like crying, I would always turn inward to one

of the stories my grandmother would read me. So as the bus drove us to *Le Chat Rouge*, I thought about Jane Austen's *Sense and Sensibility*—how after the father dies the mother and daughters are totally out of luck because the father's estate can only go to a male heir. The women are left totally out in the cold and forced to rely on the kindness of relatives.

At least I had my grandmother who gave me the gift of these stories and that gift inspired a career.

My mother would be at the mercy of the latest man in her life. I would always and forever be able to take care of myself.

As I looked around at the busload of people, I wondered if this was enough. I have people in my life. They may come and go. We share the happy moments—it struck me like a flash of lightning how my situation paralleled my mother's. The impermanence of it.

I took their money.

She took their love.

As the bus finally pulled up in front of the club, I had to admit to myself—as much as I hated the thought—maybe I was more like my mother than I cared to admit.

Yeah. Happy birthday to me.

Raoul stopped at the door to the club, letting it close behind the last of the guests. "Esme, I forgot to mention that I was successful in placing the ad in the paper. I hope we will start to receive some applications soon."

I had no idea why we had to stop and talk about this now, when we should be inside seeing to the reservation.

"That's great, Raoul. Thank you."

I turned to go inside. He caught my arm and pulled me back.

"I was thinking that if you like this place that we might make it a permanent part of the tour. I could talk to the owner and work out some sort of agreement for the steady business. Of course, my cousin and his band of gypsies would not be here every night—this is a special engagement, but come over here and look at the lineup they have posted—"

He walked over to a glass window box that housed posters and photos of various artists who were set to appear.

"Look, here is my cousin."

A mild breeze blew and flirted with the hem of my skirt. I humored him and walked over and gave the photo a cursory glance, swallowing my mounting impatience. Maybe I should've stayed home because my mood seemed to be going downhill fast.

"Great," I said, reaching down very deep inside myself and pulling up as much cheer as I could find. It wasn't very much, but it was enough to sound halfway civil when I said, "Why don't we go inside so I can meet him?"

Raoul nodded. "That's a great idea!"

I blinked at his exuberance. What in the world? Oooh, he was probably overcompensating for the fact that my mother was gone. The gentleman he was, he hadn't brought it up. Probably knowing how it would upset me....

He held open the door for me, pausing to look at a poster of his cousin's band.

"This one is Jean and this is…"

Arrrrgh! Thank God I was able to grit my teeth so the angry cry didn't slip out. I turned away from him and started walking down the red-walled entry hall before I ended up saying something I'd regret.

Raoul was on my heels.

As I reached the end of the hallway and pushed through a curtain of gold hippie beads, I saw—

My mother!

She gasped and whistled to the members of our tour group who were gathered around a long table.

The entire gang shouted, "Surprise!"

Then the band broke into a banjo, guitar and *fiddle* version of *Happy Birthday to You.*

5:00 p.m.

After we'd finished the farewell breakfast and had delivered our charges to the airport, my mother and I sat in the living room of my apartment with her luggage at her feet, drinking a bottle of champagne.

"I really thought you'd gone."

"With that man?" She curled her upper lip. "Heavens no."

I took a small sip of my drink. "But he came all this way to woo you back."

She shrugged, a faraway look in her eyes. "I told you, I should've never married him in the first place."

She'd said that several times, but I'd never asked, "Why not?"

She tipped up her glass and drank the last of the contents. "I realized sometime after he left me the second time that this relationship was no good for me. In the past I would've just picked up and left. Moved on to greener pastures. But I was tired of it. Tired of all the moving and changing. It wears on a girl after a while. I took a good look at myself and asked how it was that I'd ended up here. I mean what did I really want? You know what I found out?"

She looked at me as if she expected me to answer.

I shook my head. "What?"

"I realized I had no idea what I wanted because I had no idea who I was. I'd never been alone with myself enough to find out."

This floored me. I hated myself for it, but I never thought my mother capable of such introspection. I was speechless. So I picked up the bottle and started to refill her glass. She put her hand over the flute.

"No, you save a glass for Raoul. What time is he supposed to pick you up anyway?"

"Not until 8:00 p.m. So that's why you came to Paris? To find yourself?"

She sat back in her chair, her gaze lowered, looking contemplative. Finally she said, "I came to Paris to be with the one living person I love. The one person who has always understood me—well, I don't know if you've understood me, but you've always accepted me. Unconditionally."

White-hot waves of shock coursed through me. Did my mother just tell me she loved me? I waited for lightning to strike or the ground to shake—for the world to end. But what happened was a single tear meandered its way down my cheek.

She loved me.

That's all I needed to know.

And despite everything, I loved her—and she always knew.

"You'd better get yourself in there and get ready for your date with that handsome man. And don't feel like you have to come home tonight—"

Maybe I wouldn't.

Maybe it was okay to become just a little bit like my mother.

THE LONG DISTANCE MOTHER

PEGGY WEBB

From the Author

Dear Reader,

Sometimes a place spawns a book. That's how "The Long Distance Mother" was born. The little town of Linn, Missouri, and its lovely people so captivated me during a book tour for *Flying Lessons* and *Driving Me Crazy*, I knew I had found a story.

I pictured my character, Sara Laney, wandering the little town, buying Jergens hand lotion at the dollar store, then stopping by the charming library downstairs to chat. I saw her writing obituaries for *The Unterrified Democrat* (changed to *The Unterrified Missourian* for this book). I envisioned her hanging curtains in a cottage just up the hill from the public cemetery, where a large sign proclaims "Linn, a community walking into the future."

Of course, Sara doesn't merely walk into the future—she flies… with a little help from friends. "The Long Distance Mother" celebrates the power and beauty of female friendships and echoes my favorite theme—women who grow wings and fly.

Sara's journey is my Mother's Day gift to you. Visit my Web site www.peggywebb.com to let me know what you think and to enter my Mother's Day contest.

Happy reading!

Peggy

In memory of Mama,
who knew how to dance,
how to laugh
and how to teach a daughter to grow wings and fly.

Olivia Scott, beloved wife of Luther Scott, deceased, and mother to our own esteemed Mayor Rufus Scott, spent her entire life right here in Linn, Missouri. We all knew and loved her for her floral gifts from her garden and her generous support of the Osage County Library. But she wanted to leave us with another thought—"Don't die an unlived life. Do something unexpected that will take your breath away." Her very words. God rest her soul.

Notes for Olivia Scott's Obituary

CHAPTER 1

If there's a crown for the Queen of Ironies, that would be me, Sara Ryan Laney, hands down.

Here I am without a child to my name—or spouse either, for that matter—and a mother who might as well have been a stray cat she spent so little time at home. But I'm celebrating Mother's Day as if I expect any minute to have a loving family pop in and shower me with gifts. Yesterday I baked carrot cake in individual heart-shaped muffin tins. Hope disguised as calories.

Before I went to church this morning I left a chicken in the crock pot. When I got back I made a salad, and now I'm sitting at my dining room table eating lunch from my good china, which I reserve for special occasions.

In honor of this day I'm playing my favorite song— "Wonderful Tonight" by Eric Clapton. You might think that's a poor choice for Mother's Day, but the song is actually about people who love each other no matter what.

I'd like to think that describes my relationship with my mother to a tee, but Pearl Harbor is more like it. Just let me get my leaky boat afloat and Rosalind Ryan launches a stealth attack to blow me out of the water.

Still, every second Sunday in May, I get out my good china, put on "Wonderful Tonight" and just keep on hoping.

After I clear the table, I pick up the phone to place a long-distance call. As it rings I picture the house on the corner of Church and Walnut in Tupelo, Mississippi, where I grew up. The forsythia will be in full bloom as well as the ornamental pear tree, which gives the small brick house behind the picket fence a fairy-tale aura. Of course, if you read fairy tales, you know Grimm can scare the pants off you.

"Hello."

My mother's voice conjures images of vivid red lipstick, swingy skirts and blond hair always windblown from constant flitting about.

"Happy Mother's Day."

"Clementine, is that you?"

My visions of everything being wonderful float off in the downpour that looks as if it's trying to wash away the city.

How Mother can mistake my sensible chirp for the exotic accent of her life-long friend would be a complete puzzlement if you didn't take into account the fact that we never talk except on holidays and I haven't seen her in five years. Not because I'm a bad daughter who doesn't want to see her mother, but because my mother hardly ever keeps her feet on the ground. She's too busy amassing frequent flyer miles and getting engaged to stray men to build a relationship with her own flesh and blood.

"It's me. Sara."

"Oh. I thought you were gone."

What kind of game is she playing now? "Good grief, Mother. I've been gone for years. I just wanted to call so you'd know I'm thinking about you, that's all."

"Why don't you come over for coffee and bunnies?"

I picture my mother at her table surrounded by white rabbits in waistcoats with watches. With Rosalind, nothing would surprise me. I'll call Clementine tonight, put a spin on the story and we'll laugh about it.

"Did you say bunnies?"

"Silly you. Of course not. I said buns."

"There must be static on your end of the phone."

"Bring that man... Oh, what's his name? You know. The one with the Charley Davidson."

"The *Harley*. Mother, are you all right?"

"Of course I am. I don't know why you ask."

"I divorced Billy Joe twenty years ago and I'm not about to bring him for a visit, even if I knew where to find him. Why are you bringing him up now?"

"I don't know. I'm just in one of my moods. I hear the doorbell. Ta ta."

She hangs up before I can ask if the invitation is real. What would happen if I went home? After all these years would there be some miraculous turnaround? Would we float toward each other like kites freed by the wind or would we drift off again toward separate continents? Standing there with the dead receiver in my hand, I feel as if my boat just got torpedoed. Again.

I'm forty-five and not a single one of my dreams has come true except finally owning my own little house. It's conveniently located on Main Street just up the hill from Linn Public Cemetery, where I hope to be carried off in high style when I die with everybody saying nice things about me, including that I know every person in town by name and that I always bought Girl Scout cookies. I have a pantry full of thin mints to prove it.

My class prophecy said I would settle down in Tupelo and live there the rest of my life, but I'm the only one in my graduating class who has lived in fourteen states. It said I would have two boys and a girl—my family ideal—but all I have is a one-eyed dog of uncertain origin named Little Bit, short for Obituary, and a mother who doesn't even recognize my voice.

Furthermore, the prophecy said I would marry a salt-of-the-earth man who loved hearth and home—my dream, exactly. But what did I end up with except Billy Joe Laney who didn't love anything except his Harley and moving all over the U.S. of A. looking for the big score that never came.

The last I heard, which was the day he signed long-distance divorce papers some twenty years ago, he was in Butte, Montana.

Here's another irony: I was never voted Most Popular, but I've turned out to be the woman in Linn whose good side everybody wants to be on and the last person they want to see before they die.

Which reminds me that I can't keep standing here in my Mother-sabotaged craft. The Mayor's mother, Olivia Scott, is coming over. Yesterday she told me it was an emergency. Although she's hoping to outwit her gallstones and other rebellious bodily malfunctions till the Fourth of July so she can enjoy her daughter-in-law's crumb-top apple pie at the family picnic, she's not taking any chances. She wants to go over her obituary with me first just in case she pops off unexpectedly.

The thing that makes me so popular with the soon-to-be-deceased is that I'm conscientious about making sure they get to tell everything they want folks to know when they depart this life. Of course, people don't always have advance notice, but still I like to think I make it easier for those who do.

You'd be surprised at what people have on their minds. Last month John Brody, God rest his soul, sat right here in my little yellow kitchen that features a pink silk arrangement of petunias on the maple dinette set and told me over hazelnut coffee that he was leaving every penny he had to the animal shelter. Brody felt his dog was the only living soul who ever paid him any attention while he was alive.

"You make sure that goes in my obituary," he said. "That'll teach my selfish, greedy nephew a lesson."

I did, of course, although I softened it a bit because I don't believe in hurting feelings. So I wrote, *In honor of the love and loyalty of his pet boxer, Kathleen Turner Brody, John Brody generously leaves everything he owned to the Linn Animal Shelter. He wanted his actions to be a lesson to all of us that kindness is always rewarded.*

You can see why I'm so popular with the dying. If I were only that popular with everybody else there's no telling where I'd be right now. It gives me the shivers to think about it.

Through my pink-sprigged yellow lace curtains, I see Olivia Scott's big black Cadillac pulling into my driveway.

I put water on for hot tea, then open my front door and take her umbrella while she wipes her shoes on my mat.

It was one of the first items I bought for this house, mainly because of its spirited message, *My dog only bites visiting evangelists and skinny blondes*, which tells you exactly where I stand. I don't want anybody telling me what to believe and I don't want anybody taking away my chocolate.

Olivia and I settle down with cake and tea while I try to put her at ease and make this seem like an ordinary social call.

"Have you ever seen such rain? Yesterday it was pouring so hard I could barely see the spire of St. George's from the Loose Creek Bridge."

"If it keeps this up, the Osage River will flood its banks," she says. "Of course, I'll not likely be around to see it."

The sky lets loose another torrent, and when Olivia shivers I turn on my little gas heater. Instantly my kitchen feels like the cozy kind of place you don't ever want to leave, which is what I thought when I first saw it twenty years ago. After being dragged all over Hell's half acre by Billy Joe, I took one look at this kitchen and told him, "I'm not ever leaving here. No matter what."

Now Olivia says to me, "Sara, have you ever taken a risk so big it took your breath away?"

I shake my head. The only risk I ever took was finally giving in to Lycra, which was supposed to enhance my curves but ended up making me look like an eggplant.

"When I was seventeen," she says, "I fell madly in love with an itinerant construction worker. Joy sang through me with every breath I took. He wanted us to run away together but at the last minute I chickened out. I'd never felt anything like that before and I never have since."

"What happened to him?"

"He became Governor of Missouri." Olivia reaches across the table and puts her frail, blue-veined hand on mine. "I want my last words to this town to be *Don't die an unlived life*."

What I learn from people with everything except the soul stripped away is immeasurable. Olivia's incandescent truth fills me with wonder and a strange, restless longing.

I tell her I will most certainly take care of her wishes. After she leaves I sit in my kitchen rubbing Little Bit's ears and staring at the flame on my gas-burning heater, thinking I could fit my life into a teacup. I could live the rest of my days in my small cottage and never have to get in my car, never have to walk farther than five blocks in any direction.

Of course, you could say the same thing about everybody in Linn because this town was written up for having the longest Main Street of any town in America its size. My front yard's in the city and my backyard is in the country.

I like that. The convenience of everything I need huddled right around me and the spectacular view of river bluffs and unobstructed blue sky and rolling green pastures dotted with big, white Charolais cattle out my back window.

Still, sometimes I'll be sitting at my computer tapping away at an obituary or pouring myself a cup of coffee or folding sheets when all of a sudden I'll feel pierced, stabbed with the kind of longing that struck me when Olivia asked if I'd ever done anything that took my breath away.

The only thing that ever took my breath away was a new whitening toothpaste that made my tongue burn. I sit in the middle pew at church so I'm lost in the crowd. I arrive everywhere I go on time. I never miss deadlines. I don't go places uninvited and I don't take shortcuts and detours.

I don't even date. Oh, I did for a while after Billy Joe left, but nothing ever panned out, so I just removed myself from the social scene.

If ever anybody was fixing to die an unlived life, it's me.

Looking at the rain slashing my window I think about my mother, about the way she took to the skies when Daddy went down in his plane. He was an airline pilot and the center of her universe.

She always left me behind.

"You're in good hands," she'd say. "Clementine will take care of you."

And it was true. Still, I used to wonder why Mother had abandoned me.

But what if she wasn't running from the responsibilities of raising a child alone? What if she was looking for something to replace Jack Ryan, something else to take her breath away?

I pick up the phone, dial Tupelo, gather my courage to ask the question. It's not much, this sense of finally raising my hand in class, but maybe it's a baby step out of my teacup life.

"Mother, it's me again. Sara. There's something I want to ask you."

"Will you take me to the dance? Jack promised, but he's not back yet."

It's funny how you can be standing in the comfort of your kitchen one minute and thrown off a cliff the next. My earlier visions of my mother vanish into the nightmare of a woman who doesn't seem to know her husband has been dead for forty-one years.

As I freefall I squeeze my eyes shut, try to breathe, try to find a parachute, a safety net, a sturdy limb, anything to hold on to.

"Mother, I'm coming home."

But she's not the net I'm looking for. After we hang up I dial Tupelo again, hear Clementine's reassuring voice that echoes the accent of her Brazilian mother and the Deep South drawl of her father.

"I'm coming home to patch things up with Mother."

"It's high time," she says. "I just hope she's going to know what in the Sam Hill you're talking about."

"Why? What's going on?"

"It's not for me to say, baby girl. But I'll tell you this, if you hadn't told me you were coming home I was going to come out there and drag you here by the hair on your head."

Clementine rigs umbrellas over her birdfeeder in thunderstorms and sets house crickets free. The only danger she poses to me is that she might smother me in one of her bear hugs.

"I guess you don't want to hear what I have to say, then."

"Say it."

"Happy Mother's Day."

She hates sentimentality. In the big silence I can picture her sprawled in her red recliner contemplating the toes of her cowboy boots. She wears them with everything, even with her robe. I think she's laboring under the delusion they make her look tough.

"Sara, are you still driving like somebody shot from a cannon?"

She's caught me red-handed and I haven't even done anything yet. Driving fast is my one and only vice. Not a deliberate act, really, but a momentary unconscious flight when I leave my shackled self behind to become somebody brave and free.

"You are. If you get yourself killed I'm going to whip you."

In spite of my nagging worries, I feel better after we say goodnight, as if I've been tucked into bed with a cup of hot chocolate. If I'd had children, I would want to be exactly like Clementine Carmita George.

Except maybe for the cowboy boots.

Everybody will remember Miss Lula Bell Franks as the librarian who opened the world of *Nancy Drew* and the *Hardy Boys* to us. Before she passed on she said her biggest regret was that she never learned to dance.
Obituary for Lula Bell Franks

Flying is an extravagance I can't afford, so the Tuesday following Mother's Day I load my bags and Little Bit then strike out on a ten-hour journey in my maroon Dodge Ram Charger that looks like I mean business. It's my alter ego. If I ever come back as a truck I want it to be a four-wheel drive with a souped-up engine and spinner hubcaps.

Nobody knows this about me except maybe Clementine. Everybody around Linn views me as a delicate but rather plain flower of Southern womanhood—average height, average looks and average brown hair—a black-eyed Susan among flamboyant day lilies.

Yesterday when I told my editor at the paper I'd be leaving for a few days you'd have thought I was going to climb Mount Everest. Larry Brody is the old-fashioned fatherly type who sees women as needing protectors. He has taken a personal interest in me ever since I did such a good job making his deceased brother John look like a philanthropist instead of a vengeful old coot.

"Don't pick up any hitchhikers and don't eat at truck stops. If anybody dies I'll call and you can e-mail the obituary."

I'd take that to mean I'm indispensable at the paper, but modesty is my middle name. If I ever had any grandiose opinions of myself, Mother disabused me of them when Daddy fell out of the sky over the Atlantic Ocean.

I was four and couldn't understand why he didn't come back, much less why my Mother flew off without me and thought postcards from Paris made up for bedtime stories and missing my birthday.

Now I say, "If I keep thinking like this I'll turn the car around and head back to our little cocoon."

I talk to my dog a lot. He perks up his ears, and gives me a lopsided canine smile while I reach over and turn on the car's radio. My favorite gospel song, "Leaning on the Everlasting Arms," is playing. It makes me think of the Universe as a compassionate mother welcoming you to her rocking chair.

My voice is not much, but I sing along anyway. If there's one thing I know, it's the words to every song in the Cokesbury hymnal. Say *church* and you'll be describing my entire social life.

Fortunately Little Bit's the only one who hears. Or unfortunately. Whichever way you want to look at it.

These songs get me all the way across Missouri and Arkansas and across the Mississippi River Bridge into Tennessee. The first time I ever crossed this bridge I was a bride of eighteen riding on the back of Billy Joe's Harley, if you can imagine me in such a position.

Or any other position for that matter. Not that I don't want somebody: I'm picky. Always have been, always will be. Most folks didn't think Billy Joe was much to pick, but he was the whipped cream on my cherry pie, and besides that, he was my ticket to permanence.

We were going to settle in Little Rock and open a used music shop. Our starter stock would be my collection of Elvis and Tammy Wynette and his stash of the Beatles. Billy Joe was going to call our store the Little Rock and Roll.

Of course, we never had a store by that or any other name, and I guess if I hadn't finally found my stubborn streak and my calling at the same time I'd still be traipsing around the country on the back of his Harley.

In order to get some continuity in my life, I'd started keeping little journals. When we ended up in Linn and I saw the opening for an obituary writer, I knew I'd met my destiny.

Plus, I just liked the name of the paper—*The Unterrified Missourian*. Seems like I'd been terrified all my life, and all of a sudden I had a chance to walk through a door every day that declared otherwise.

As I make the last turn out of Memphis and head down Highway 78 toward home, I pretend I'm walking through that door. Unterrified.

That's me, pretending.

TWO HOURS LATER I'm wheeling along McCullough Boulevard on the outskirts of Tupelo. Once a long stretch of road with a few houses, a truck stop and a grocery store that served ice cream dipped from big buckets in the freezer, it has turned into a strip of businesses and service stations with one or two holdouts still living in houses shuttered against the roar of traffic.

I wonder what changes I'll see in my old neighborhood. In my mother.

I exit onto Jackson, swing around behind Church Street Elementary School and approach from the back. Every light in the house is on and the front yard is ablaze with torches. The kind you see on patios and in restaurants that want to make you think you're on the beach in Hawaii.

At first I think Mother's having a party, but when I park I see there's not another car in sight, not even Mother's treasured vintage Thunderbird convertible. Still, maybe it's a block party. Maybe everybody walked.

Leaving my suitcases in the car I weave my way among the

gardenia and camellia bushes toward the front yard with Little Bit at my heels. Am I hearing bells or is there merely a ringing in my ears? Is it some strange side effect of travel fatigue?

When I round the corner the bells become distinctive and I stop, stunned. They're on Mother's black skirt, sewn on haphazardly with bright red thread. Her face is lifted to the moon, rapt, and her arms curve outward as if she's waltzing with a partner instead of twirling around her front yard alone.

Standing on the outskirts of the yard I feel like a little girl with her face pressed to the ballroom window. I have the strongest feeling that my mother used to dance like this all the time, that I used to dance with her, the two of us caught up in a whirlwind of bright color and music and laughter.

What would happen if I could cross the yard and dance with her? Would I become part of her world, a colorful, international-flavored world that used to bedazzle me? I'll never know because correct behavior is my other middle name. I don't want to do anything to make a fool of myself, and I most certainly don't want to be somebody's juicy gossip over morning coffee.

Like a bird dog trained to stand at attention, pointing while the birds fly around having all the fun, I wait for Mother to stop dancing and notice me. I excel at this. I've been waiting for her to notice me all my life.

Her bright red lipstick has escaped its bounds and overflows the corners of her mouth. The carefree hair of my memories is an unkempt topknot of washed-out blond streaked with gray. Rosalind Ryan strikes me as a faded home movie instead of a person.

And I don't think she's ever going to look my way and say, "Oh, there you are," as if seeing me is the most exciting part of her day.

I call out *Mother*, but she either doesn't hear me or doesn't pay me any attention, which is not news. I go over and stand in front of her, my hands folded as if I've brought an offering.

Or a sacrifice. Goose bumps pop up along my arm and I pull my sweater close.

"What are you doing dressed like this?"

Her look of rapture wavers then disintegrates. "Don't you like my bells?"

She sounds like a six-year-old caught pulling the cat's tail instead of the woman who once dined in Rome with the great tenor Pavarotti.

"I'm sure they're the rage abroad." In Tupelo where your business is everybody's, the neighbors will be talking. "Let's go in the house."

She had been dancing with the grace of a prima ballerina, but now she stumbles along like a woman of eighty-five instead of twenty years younger. When I take hold of her elbow I notice the powdery texture of her skin, the way it hangs on her bones, the scent of bacon grease clinging to her hair.

The mother I knew in brief fits and spurts was fastidious about her appearance. The last time I saw her, she was wearing a yellow linen dress and a wide-brimmed Italian straw hat she'd bought in Milan. It was Clementine's sixtieth birthday and Mother had flown in for the party bearing a tapestry older than Boston and a man younger than my tennis shoes. The tapestry featured an embroidered unicorn that fit right into Clementine's unicorn collection. The man didn't fit anywhere.

Without advance preparation, Mother said, "Sara, meet the man who's going to be your father."

Even tornadoes give warnings.

"I never had a mother," I said. "Why would I need a father?"

As I evacuated I heard Clementine tell her, "Good grief, Rosalind, what did you want her to do? Kiss his hand or potty train him?"

I never did know what happened to him. Clementine says he probably drowned in his Pablum. All I know is that my mother never married him and I quit coming home. It was the only way I knew to keep my own war-torn, patched-up craft afloat.

As much as Clementine loved me, she was too busy making a living to fill all the gaps Mother left behind. I grew up with an unspeakable secret: I was not good enough to make a mother want to stay. Now, here I am, back home and feeling like that little girl again.

The house has changed little since I last saw it—Grand-mother Ryan's antique lamps and marble-topped tables add the grace and charm lacking in the functional brown velvet sofa and side chairs, the fat ottoman, the nondescript hooked rug. Everything is pristine.

Clementine's doings? Housekeeping was another nuisance Mother avoided.

"Clementine brought roast beef, if you want it."

"Have you eaten?"

Mother frowns as if I've asked her to recite the Declaration of Independence. Then she waves her hand and says, "Sometimes these TV shows can drive you crazy."

"What TV shows?"

"Oh, you know. About roast beef."

"Julia Child? Martha Stewart?"

"Yes, where they do all that...." She makes stirring motions. "Do you like roast beef? Clementine comes over every day with a pot. She makes it and goes in and out the door. In and out, in and out."

Mother's hands flutter about like birds caught in a net, and I feel as if I've stopped breathing. When I set out this morning I knew I was leaving safe territory, but I never figured on landing on the moon.

The air is too thin in this house, the loss of gravity so severe I feel untethered, a woman floating off into wide, blue un-charted spaces without the least idea how to get home again.

Breathe, I tell myself. Just breathe.

Little Bit goes over to press his soft muzzle against Mother's leg and she settles down, looks as if she's found some peaceful place inside herself. Sometimes I think dogs are angels. I think they're the wisest creatures I know.

As I capture Mother's hands in mine, I think how fragile life is, like a beating heart held in the open palm of your hand.

"Shhh. It's all right, Mother. Everything will be all right."

I wish I believed this were true. I wish I were the kind of woman who could make it true.

If you ever attended a summer fair at the park on Highway 50 you'll remember Vera Leslie's chicken salad. She was famous for it. She was also famous for taking in strays—dogs, cats, teenaged runaways, strangers down on their luck. She was an angel to them all.

Obituary for Vera Lee Leslie

CHAPTER 3

I'm about to fall asleep sitting in the chair at Mother's doctor's office waiting to find out if Mother's antics signal disease or if they are merely part of her latest game.

She seemed perfectly normal this morning asking questions about my job. When I left to visit her doctor she was watching TV with Little Bit sitting in her lap. Still, I wasn't sure leaving her alone was the right thing to do.

I don't think Mother slept two winks last night. Even when I didn't hear her up prowling the kitchen at all hours, I lay awake wondering what she'd do next—go skinny-dipping in the neighbor's pool or snatch my car keys and drive to Nantucket to see the whales. If she ran off, it would be to do something wildly adventurous.

I wonder why all her brave and daring genes passed me by?

Maybe I'm adopted and she never told me. Maybe she never will, because when the receptionist calls me back and I sit in the leather chair in front of Dr. Ruben Simmons's desk, he tells me, "In February, I made a definitive diagnosis. Your mother's in the early stages of Alzheimer's."

They call this disease the long goodbye. What they don't know is that I said goodbye to my mother when she got on her first overseas flight, and I've been saying goodbye to her ever since.

"Your mother's still fairly functional, and Miss George has been doing a great job, but eventually Rosalind will need full-time care."

Dr. Simmons slides brochures on the area's nursing homes across the desk and I stick them into my purse without looking. Thank you seems inappropriate in this situation, and, besides, my throat has closed and I can't talk.

He hands me a tissue and I wipe my face. I don't know why I'm crying. It's not as if I'm losing something. You can't lose something you never had in the first place.

Maybe I'm crying for myself. Selfish me. The little girl who never was. Clementine says I was born with the Golden Rule tattooed on my backside and a Social Security application clutched in my hand. In other words, old. And boring.

When I leave the doctor's office, I don't scout the nursing

homes because it doesn't seem right to arrive one day and cram my mother in one the next.

I suspect the truth goes a bit deeper, but I'm not prepared to go digging around in my own motives. My life is carefully constructed, neat and socially correct. I plan to keep it that way.

What I do, instead, is call Mother.

"What are you doing?" I try to sound casual, not like a daughter with a time bomb now attached to the hull of her leaky boat.

"Watching TV. I like the soap operas."

This sounds normal enough. I feel free to go by Wal-Mart after I hang up and purchase a few groceries plus eight six-packs of Hershey's bars with almonds and six pots of pink azaleas. Then I drive straight to the familiar stucco cottage on Madison Street. It's smaller than most of the surrounding houses, distinctive because of its Southwestern flavor and a bit exotic. It suits Clementine George to a tee.

The first thing I see is Mother's prized Thunderbird.

Before I'm even out of my truck Clementine prances across the yard in her cowboy boots and tight blue jeans, never mind that she now has a spare tire that folds over her hand-tooled leather belt. The top buttons on her hot pink cowboy shirt are straining against the weight of a bosom grown large enough to enfold Texas.

"I guess you're going to ask what I'm doing with Rosalind's car."

Clementine's offhand greeting doesn't fool me.

"Yes, I suppose I am." I kiss her on the cheek, try to act as nonchalant as she, try not to stare at the car.

Daddy bought the Thunderbird the week before his plane went down, and ever after, Mother treated it like a favored child. I can't imagine her parting with it.

"She asked me to keep it here."

"Why?"

"She ran a red light and knocked down the sandwich board sign in front of the new tattoo parlor. I told her it was an eyesore anyway and needing knocking down."

Feeling as if somebody has put a long, angry scratch on me instead of the car, I turn away quickly and start unloading pots of azaleas.

"If you're trying to bribe me, Sara, it's working."

"I'm trying to thank you. Or maybe it's just guilt talking. How long have you been taking care of Mother, and why didn't you tell me?"

"About six months and I promised Rosalind I wouldn't tell."

"Were you just going to keep on?"

"As long as I could hold out."

"I don't know why. Mother's never done a single thing except use you for a babysitter."

"She gave me more than you can imagine."

I certainly can't imagine it and don't want to. I just want to find a place for this mother I hardly know and get back to the peace and security of my small cottage.

As I help Clementine plant the azaleas, I bury more than my hands in the dirt: I bury nagging questions and guilt and sadness at coming home to something that's not even there.

As we head to Clementine's kitchen to wash up, I see yards of lace and satin curled around her sewing room—the tender mercies of my childhood. I used to spend hours at her feet while she stitched evening gowns, dance costumes, and couture-worthy suits for Tupelo's upper crust. Wrapping myself in a length of pink satin, I would pretend I was in Paris or Brussels or whatever foreign city happened to be my mother's current favorite. When I would tell Clementine my fantasy, she'd burst into song, making up words that put me at the heart and center of Mother's adventures.

"How about tea and cookies?" Clementine says.

"I can't. I have milk in the car."

I hold her close and thank her for taking care of Rosalind, and she tells me to keep my lead foot off the gas pedal.

When I get pulled over for speeding I wish I'd taken her advice. Wouldn't you know it's a motorcycle cop? Still, he's about my own age, maybe a bit younger, somebody who might understand I'm not being reckless, I'm just trying to fly off and leave the creaky hull of my life behind.

"I'm sorry, Officer Hogan." I use the name on his badge, hoping it will help my cause. "I guess I thought I was somebody else." Meaning brave.

"Who? Jeff Gordon?"

To say I'm terrible at small talk is the world's biggest understatement. But his ordinary, down-to-earth looks and his good-natured laugh makes me feel bolder than my usual self.

"Going a few miles over the limit makes me feel...oh, I don't know. Free."

He writes the ticket anyway. I never did have much luck with a man on a Harley.

"There's a racetrack on the south side of town you might want to try. But slow it down a bit on the streets. Okay, Ms. Laney?"

I inch home chastened but unreformed. Except for this one little vice, my behavior is practically perfect, and perfection is even more boring than being the upright woman I am.

Or is that only what I've become?

WHEN I GET HOME, Mother is still watching TV, her hands rubbing Little Bit's fur, her feet crossed at the ankles like a perfect lady. She's exactly as I left her except for one glaring difference. Her pajama bottoms are on her head, the elastic waist stretched across her forehead, the legs tied under her chin like a bonnet.

Until that moment I didn't know it was possible for a

virtual stranger to break your heart. While I'm standing there trying not to cry again and wondering how I'm supposed to handle this, she looks up at me and smiles.

"I dressed for bed."

I sit beside her, take her hand, clear my throat, act as if silk pajama bottoms should become hats.

"I see that. Have you had a good day?"

"That lady who goes in and out brought a...this big round...thing. Full of brown...you know, that stuff."

"Your friend? Clementine?"

She nods. "My dark-eyed friend."

I unload groceries then go into the kitchen and see a chocolate cake on Clementine's footed glass cake stand. Beside it is a bowl of grapes that wasn't there when I left. In the refrigerator I find a platter of pimento cheese sandwiches and a huge casserole that looks like Clementine's famous chicken concoction.

There's no telling what else she did while she was here, what she's been doing for Mother every day since she found out. And without a word to me, without any thought of being acknowledged for her kindness, without any complaint that in addition to taking care of herself she's taking care of somebody else who is not even family.

My closest connection is my dog. I can't imagine a friendship that inspires this kind of loyalty, this kind of compassion.

After I stow groceries, I carry sandwiches, iced tea and cake into the living room and set up the plates on TV trays.

"I thought you might enjoy having lunch in here." Mother stares at her food, unmoving, then at me as I bite into a sandwich. "Aren't you hungry? Go ahead and eat. You like pimento cheese."

"Yes, Bob makes cheese." She picks her sandwich then mimics every movement I make while she chatters, animated, about a man I never heard of, one who might be real only in her mind and whose sole purpose in life apparently was making Rosalind Ryan laugh about cheese.

She seems happy in this fantasy, and I sit beside her the rest of the afternoon, nodding and laughing, while she rattles on. I don't know if this is the right thing to do, but it keeps her content.

By the time dark comes and I've coached her through another meal, I'm exhausted. I lead her to the bedroom and try to convince her to let me convert the pajamas to sleepwear. But she gets so agitated I cave in and let her go to bed wearing them on her head.

When I leave, Little Bit stays on the small Oriental rug beside her bed as if he understands how she needs him.

I stand in the door a while, watching to make sure she's asleep then go into the kitchen to make myself a cup of good strong coffee.

If I were home I'd be making my favorite green tea chai

full of rich cream and spices, but I'll make do with a cup of Colombian. I feel the need to settle into a quiet corner and center myself, listen to my own instincts. I think that's just another word for angels, really, and I think we don't let ourselves be still long enough to hear them, let alone understand the wisdom of their messages.

I open the canister, put the scoop in and bring up a note bearing my name. Shaking off the coffee grounds, I begin to read.

"Sara, I don't know how much time I have to say this. My mind comes and goes. Mostly it goes."

Mother has drawn a smiley face here. Before Daddy died, she put them on every crayon drawing I made then hung them on the refrigerator with magnets shaped like stars.

"I know you think I haven't done right by you, but Clementine and Jack were always the ones suited to parenthood. You have to understand this. You must. I could not..."

Mother's writing suddenly goes wobbly and veers off into gibberish. I hide the note in my pocket then make coffee.

Why didn't she tell me these things years ago when both of us might have been able to salvage something of this war-torn relationship?

While the coffee's brewing I open the cabinets and find another note tucked inside a ceramic mug bearing a miniature replica of the Mona Lisa. A fitting hiding place since this note is even more inscrutable than the first.

"Love is not a bird, Sara, it's a tree. If you could understand the tree, you'd know. I should have told you why we did it. I should have let you see for yourself. Find the tree. Ask Clementine. She can…"

The sentence trails off into a series of Xs and Os that snake around the spidery handwriting then fall off the page. A child's symbols for hugs and kisses. Was my mother trying to tell me that she loves me?

My need for strong coffee vanishes in the face of my need to understand the notes. What secrets is Mother keeping, and if I discover them, will I also discover her?

With the rich, dark smells of Colombian coffee swirling around me, I fish the other note out of my pocket and read them both again. They carry no dates, only a sense of urgency.

I imagine Mother snatching her moments of lucidity, scribbling furiously before her mind wandered off once more into the fog of Alzheimer's. Stuffing them back into my pocket, I pick up the phone and call Clementine.

"I can't put Mother in a nursing home."

"I know, baby girl."

"We have to talk."

"Whenever you're ready."

"I have to go home first, tend to some business in Linn. I don't know how long it will take."

"Take your time. I'll be here. I'll take care of Rosalind till you get back."

I will probably always associate the smell of coffee with the moment I fell from sanity. *Taking care of business* means selling my house, quitting my job, pulling up roots, undoing everything I've spent my whole life working for.

Does falling out of sanity mean I've fallen into something better? Does it mean I've fallen into grace? As the word whispers through my mind, I grab hold, anchoring myself.

"There's only one thing I want people to know. Life's no picnic. You might as well laugh and spend your money. You sure can't take it with you. They won't even let me be buried in my Cadillac."

From the Obituary of Jim Fields

CHAPTER 4

I come out of a deep sleep with the vague sense that I've lost something and my dog is trying to notify me from a distance. When the doorbell rings, I realize I'm not dreaming; it's 2:00 a.m., I'm in Mother's house with her cryptic notes on the bedside table, and Little Bit is barking outside the door. I fling it open and walk into my own nightmare.

The motorcycle cop who gave me a speeding ticket is standing on the front porch holding my mother's arm while Little Bit does a whirling dervish dance around them, yapping.

"Ms. Laney?"

When somebody remembers you, it makes you feel important. Expansive, even. No matter what the circumstances.

"Call me Sara."

"Does this woman live here?"

"Yes. She's my mother."

Suddenly I'm reduced to a woman who plunges from one crisis to the next because she's not alert, not paying attention. A big, fat failure who sleeps while her mother sneaks off to get run over or mugged or kidnapped.

"She was wandering around the library parking lot with this little dog. I live in the apartment building next door, and this wee fellow's yapping alerted me." Just a few blocks, thank goodness. Still, I shiver to think what might have happened.

"I have to see Pat Conroy." Imparting this chunk of her past, Mother acts as imperious as Marie Antoinette. "We're having lunch after his speech and we're going to discuss living in Rome."

She sends a look at Officer Hogan that suggests guillotines in his immediate future.

I'm big on finding the silver lining, but so far the only positive side I can see is that Mother is not wearing her pajamas on her head. Before she sneaked out she dressed to the nines—purse, hat, shoes, even a designer suit fit for lunch with the First Lady.

"She wouldn't tell me her name and wouldn't show me her driver's license, so I followed the little dog."

Mother fishes something out of her purse and hands it to him.

"Here's a picture of Jesus. Will that do?"

It's a daily devotional book with tattered edges.

Officer Hogan's eyes crinkle up at the corners and I can see he's trying not to laugh. All of a sudden I explode. I don't know whether this fit of guffawing is going to make me die of embarrassment or whether it has saved me.

When Officer Hogan and Mother join in, I catch a glimpse of how we can survive this long goodbye: find humor wherever we can. Take the worst possible situation and tame it with laughter into something that won't break your heart and trample your spirit.

"Thank you for bringing her home. Won't you come in? I can make coffee." It seems the least I can do.

"I'll have to take a rain check, but I'd love it some other time. You ladies have a good night and call me if you need me."

He hands me his card with a telephone number and his name. Mick. Nice Irish name that suits his red hair and his big, booming laugh.

After he leaves, I try to lead Mother back to bed, but she thinks she's still having lunch with Pat Conroy, that he'll be here any minute and she'll miss him if she falls asleep.

Besides that, she's wound up and pleased with herself that she's the center of attention and the life of the party.

"That man in the hat laughed and laughed and laughed."

"Yes, he did, Mother."

"I danced."

"When?"

"With Pat. And that man."

"The one in the hat? Officer Hogan?"

"I don't think he has an office. He walked. We walked together. Tra la la. Singing."

She bursts into a song that sounds like opera and sounds like Italian, but what do I know? Gospel. That's what. Cast your burdens and count your blessings. In good, plain English, please.

Little Bit lies down across the top of my feet and I have to fight to keep my eyes open and my body semi-alert. If I'm not vigilant, Mother will escape again.

How am I ever going to prevent it? Take vitamins, for one thing. I'm a firm believer in eating right, exercising and taking vitamins.

Forget plenty of rest. That's not going to happen. At least, not till I figure out how I'm going to keep Mother from becoming Houdini, the escape artist.

IN LIGHT OF MOTHER'S great escape, as I'm now referring to it, I call Clementine at seven o'clock. She's a creature of habit. By now she's had her first cup of coffee and she's sitting in front of the TV with her second cup watching the *Today Show*.

When I relay the current news of Rosalind, the runaway, she says, "Don't you worry about a thing. I'll pack a bag and stay with her while you're gone. When are you leaving?"

"Not till after I've had a nap. I'm liable to fall asleep and run off the road."

"What's she doing now?"

"She's still sitting on the sofa in her hat and suit chattering about having lunch. She's moved on from Pat Conroy to a former governor of Mississippi and the sexiest movie star alive."

"She had lunch with both of them. George was in Mississippi making a film."

Will I ever find out all there is to know about this mysterious woman who dines with governors and movie stars?

"I'm coming over, Sara. I'll give you the key to my house and you can sleep as long as you need to."

I don't know what I'd do without Clementine.

BACK HOME IN MISSOURI it seems impossible that only yesterday I was in Tupelo with a mother who dresses in Chanel to run away. While Little Bit runs around the fenced-in backyard chasing squirrels, I walk through my house deciding what to sell and what to keep.

There's no use duplicating tables, beds, nightstands, rocking chairs, but as I tape "sell" tags on my furniture I remember my first cup of coffee with Billy Joe at the maple dinette set, the first night in the cherry four-poster bed, the first set of dishes we bought. I thought he'd settle down and we'd go on that way forever. I thought we'd have coffee at that same table fifty years later when our children and grandchildren brought over chocolate cherry cake to cele- brate our anniversary.

Tradition. Roots. Progeny. That's what I wanted.

For a moment I stand with my hand over my heart as if somebody's trying to rip it out by the roots. Then I remember that none of this is durable goods so I might as well quit acting as if I'm destroying Rome and get on with it.

THE HARDEST PART of leaving Linn comes the next day when I say goodbye to friends. Actually *acquaintances* is a better term, because I was so busy staying safe in my cocoon I never let anybody get close enough to call me up in the middle of the night and say, *Can you come over and sit in the middle of my bed and eat buttered popcorn and Hershey's bars? I need chocolate and butter and talk, in that order.*

After I list my house with a Realtor, I pick up cleaning supplies at the Dollar General Store then pop downstairs to the library in the basement. Besides my colleagues at the *Unterrified Missourian*, this is my hardest goodbye. I'll miss Judy Finney and her staff, but most of all I'll miss sitting near the front entrance surrounded by the orderly stacks, smelling the dusty scent of books and watching the sky change colors.

In Linn I can walk out of the library or the grocery store or the offices of the newspaper and know I'm heading into a haven where my little dog is waiting with his tail wagging, his ears perked and his tongue hanging out. Home, that's what I head toward.

And now I'm pulling up stakes and heading toward the unknown.

Mark Gibson was best known for his generous support of Linn Public Schools, the pumpkin patch on his farm that he opened to children every fall and his Cuban cigar. But here's what he wanted all his friends and neighbors to understand: "I grew up dirt poor in Tunica, Mississippi, picking cotton on somebody else's farm. Never forget your roots. They make you who you are. From the Obituary of Mark Gibson

CHAPTER 5

When you live the kind of quiet, narrow life I have, it doesn't take long to leave. Two weeks after I left Tupelo, I'm headed back, Little Bit in the passenger seat and the back end of my pickup loaded with the few possessions I wanted to keep: my whistling teakettle, my china tea set, my favorite brass lamp featuring cherubs on the base and eight boxes of books, which just goes to show the kind of person I am.

No wonder I split with Billy Joe. He never did like to read. I guess if he had I'd still be traveling all over the country on the back of his Harley, dragging my maple dinette set along in a trailer.

I wonder if Officer Mick Hogan likes to read. If he has to rescue Mother again I might lend him my copy of Robert Frost's Poems, point out my favorite, "The Cow in Apple Time."

"Why?" he might ask, and I'll tell him I identify with the cow that got drunk on overripe apples and finally leaped over boundaries in her tipsy carouse.

Of course, I don't drink and in my current situation I'm not likely to go leaping over any boundaries. I'll probably be standing guard at the doors and windows while Mother uses me for target practice.

WHEN I SEE HER, I feel guilty for thinking of her as the strong-willed, self-absorbed woman whose sole reaction to me has always been attack, subdue and retreat.

Mother's sitting on the sofa with my childhood Raggedy Ann cradled in her arms, humming, while Clementine sits in the rocking chair beside her, crocheting.

"Have you met my little daughter?" Mother bends over the doll. "Where are your manners, Sara? Say hello to the nice lady."

"She's been like this for three days. Won't let that doll out of her sight." Clementine puts her sewing in a basket then hugs me. "Are you okay?"

This is not a question about my health. She's asking how

I feel about leaving behind my real life and walking into the upheaval of Mother's fantasy world.

"I am."

"I knew my baby girl would come through."

Clementine always makes me want to lean on her and forget about everything except the comfort and security of her embrace. But she has fatigue lines around her mouth and gray streaks in her hair and I'm no longer a child. It's high time to reverse roles.

"After I get Mother to bed, I need to go over her financial records. Do you know where she keeps them?"

"In your father's desk, same as always, and I can tell you right now that, in spite of my advice, Rosalind spent his life insurance money like it was oil and she was a rich Texan."

"Meaning I need to be looking for work?"

"Depends on how high on the hog you want to live. By the way, that nice Officer Hogan stopped by to check on you."

"He came here to see about Mother?"

"He asked about both of you. If you ask me, he was disappointed to find me here instead of you."

It's funny how such a small thing can make you feel as if you've just had a massage and your hair freshly done. Good all over. Little prickles of pleasure running down your spine.

Maybe my intense reaction to a simple inquiry has nothing to do with Officer Hogan's friendly manner and everything to do with my circumstances: a woman with no job and an uncertain future suddenly thrust into full-time care giving.

After Clementine leaves, Mother is tucked into bed with her doll and the doors and windows are securely fastened, I sit at Daddy's desk to compare ways with means.

If I live frugally, which is a given considering my lifestyle of the past forty-five years, I can stay here with Mother full time for at least two years without having to work. An alternate plan would be to find a job and hire a sitter during the day. That seems the more sensible plan. Otherwise I'll be forced to watch my nest egg and Mother's savings flow out the door in a non-replenishable stream.

When I call to tell Clementine my plan, I get a taste of the flash-fire temper that kept me out of the street with my jump rope at six and out of cars with strange boys at sixteen.

"What do you mean, hire a sitter? I'm perfectly capable of taking care of Rosalind."

"You spent the first part of your life taking care of me. I'm not going to let you spend the last half taking care of my mother."

"You and which army are going to keep me from it?"

Down the hall I hear Little Bit yip and Mother stumbling out of bed.

"I've got to go. We'll discuss this later."

"You bet your sweet britches, we will."

I race to the bedroom to find her searching the closet.

"Mother, what are you doing?"

"I can't find my ballet slippers."

"You don't have any ballet slippers. Let me help you back to bed."

"No." She shakes my hand off her arm and looks at me as if I've tried to hog-tie her. "What are you doing in my house? I'm telling my daughter."

"Mother, I am your daughter. I'm Sara, remember?"

Confusion clouds her face, then she draws herself up and gives me an arch look.

"Young lady, get to bed this minute or I'm calling your daddy."

Now what? Day one of my new life and already I'm wishing I could run away to Mexico and chug tequila. And me, not even a drinker.

"Don't call Daddy. I think he flew to Amsterdam. Let's just sit on the bed and read stories."

I grab the closest book I can find, a copy of Pat Conroy's *Prince of Tides* from the bookshelves across the room. I know it's one of Mother's favorites and know it's signed, but I don't know when and how.

Tomorrow I'll ask Clementine. Tomorrow I'll ask her lots of things.

Mother takes the book, studies the first page and moves her mouth silently. In the same way you discover someone has broken into your house and stolen everything you cherish, I realize that Mother can no longer read. Whether the condition is temporary or permanent, I don't know.

All I know is that when I take the book and start to read, she settles against the pillows, smiling.

"Read the part about the whales," she says, and I know that somewhere in the dark reaches of her dimming mind still lie the memories of foreign cities and unforgettable moments, great books and grand passion. Somewhere beyond my reach or hers, Mother is still the Rosalind Ryan who inspired the loyalty of a man who loved her beyond reason and a friend who would sacrifice her life for her.

I wonder if I'll ever know that Rosalind Ryan, and if, in discovering her, I can discover myself.

Am I merely this tepid woman focused on writing about the dead, or is there an interesting, lusty-for-life Sara hidden inside just waiting for me to set her free?

After she falls asleep I start toward my own bedroom but it's only nine o'clock. Nighttimes are always the loneliest. I feel as if I'm stranded in the Sahara surrounded by vast, unchanging stretches of sand. No relief in sight. Just the relentless march of time and the certainty that I'll recede further into my shell if I don't find somebody—meaning somebody besides my dog and my barely here mother, somebody like Officer Hogan, who wasn't wearing a ring.

Searching my purse I find the card. If I think too much about this, I'll never call. I'll start thinking he surely has a woman in his life, so why should I bother. Finally I just pick up the phone and dial.

"Officer Hogan? Mick? I was wondering if you're free for that cup of coffee? I even have chocolate cake."

"Just give me a minute to change. I've been in the garage installing shelves for my fishing gear."

"Take your time. I'm not going anywhere."

Thirty minutes later he's standing at my front door in jeans and a crisp white shirt open at the neck and rolled at the sleeves. His face has the freshly polished look of a man who just shaved and he's wearing a hint of woodsy scent.

Men don't dress for me. They don't shave and they certainly don't wear aftershave. If it weren't for the bits of sawdust clinging to his hair I'd be intimidated. I grin as if I've won a weekend getaway to Hot Springs, Arkansas.

"What? Do I have shaving cream behind my ear?"

"No. Sawdust."

"I like to putter around when I come home. It relaxes me."

"I hope you like strong coffee."

"The stronger the better."

I lead him into the kitchen and imagine myself discovering that he likes his women with a little meat on their bones, built for comfort not speed. I picture him revealing he's never wanted a woman who spends more time putting on her makeup than she does reading the morning paper, that if he had a choice he'd pick a plain woman over a pretty one every time because the beautiful ones tend to spend more time at the mall than they do in the couch cuddled up watching the baseball playoffs.

"I like baseball," I tell Mick over cake and coffee, and he quirks his eyebrow upward.

"Do you read minds? I was pitcher at U.T."

Turns out, he has lots of connections to Tennessee—an ex-wife who hated his job, twin boys getting ready for their freshman year at college, a mother who trains and shows Tennessee walking horses.

He has this rich history that fills the kitchen with color and excitement. Ordinarily I'd feel drab, compared. But I don't. I feel comfortable, so relaxed I don't even hear noises.

"Is that your mother?" Mick says.

I jump as if I've been shocked with a cattle prod.

"Oh, Lord. I have to go."

"Let me help."

All of a sudden I want to cry. Unexpected kindness does this to me.

"Mother had a sister with Alzheimer's." Mick reaches out and rubs my upper arm. "Come on, Sara. Tonight you don't have to do this alone."

He leads me down the hall, holding my hand, and I am unutterably grateful.

It's not the big moments that rescue us; it's life's small, tender mercies.

"Everybody's going to wonder why I'm being buried by Wanda Easley instead of my deceased husband. I'm not one to speak ill of the dead. All I'm going to say is that if it hadn't been for Wanda's friendship, I'd have given up and kicked the bucket a long time ago."
From the Obituary of Martha Vail

CHAPTER 6

The first thing I do when I wake up is check on Mother. She's still sleeping, thank goodness, Little Bit on the rug beside her and the Pat Conroy book open on her bedside to the passage about whales.

Later, in the bathroom reaching for a towel, I figure *built for comfort* won't describe me, but *whale* will if I don't find a way to resist Clementine's chocolate cakes. As I drag the towel from the shelf, a note flutters to the ground.

"Dear Sara, I'm careless with living things, even pets. My cat Moonlight escaped with a big tom, my dog Rascal ran away to find an owner who would take him for regular walks and save him the embarrassment of peeing on the rug and my goldfish would have turned belly up in putrid water if Clementine hadn't been there to save them.

"She saved us all. She's God's gift to us and my gift to you. She's our star, the one we look to when we're lost and need to find our way. With much love and towels and water and Tootsie Rolls and ostrich plumes and…"

The list goes on, reminding me that mere words cannot tell the story of a life. But words arranged in a hammer stroke of truth can strike sparks on a heart and shape a future different from the one we conceive with our limited imaginations.

I must talk to Clementine. I dress quickly and am reaching for the phone when the doorbell rings. The Latin Hurricane, herself, sweeps past me then plunks a tray and her boots on the coffee table.

"I brought sausages and biscuits. Get some coffee. We're fixing to talk and it's either going to be heart to heart or knock down and drag out. It's all up to you."

"Good morning, Clementine."

"You can't sweet-talk me. Just pour the coffee."

Little Bit wanders into the kitchen while Clementine's in the den belting out, "Get out of my way; don't you mess with me. The last one who did is hangin' from a tree." She's about as subtle as a bulldozer mowing down a petunia bed.

I measure coffee into the filter and dog food into Little Bit's dish, then wait for the dark brew to fill the glass canister.

"I hope it's good and strong," Clementine says when I return, then passes the biscuits. "I married a jackass."

Before I can ask what in the world her ex-husband has to do with Mother, she waves her hand for me to sit down, shut up and listen.

"Rosalind warned me. But I didn't listen. I was twenty and in lust and wild horses couldn't have kept me out of Jerry George's pants."

I've barely readjusted my image of Clementine from earth mother to hot tamale when she drops another bomb.

"I couldn't have kids. Jerry said he was okay with that, but six months after the wedding he left me for a floozy as fertile as a doe rabbit in a blackberry patch."

She takes a bite of biscuit and a sip of coffee while I wait. It's one thing I'm very good at.

"It happens all the time," she said. "But mix Latin blood with drama and you get somebody who wanted to mutilate his gene pool with a dull pair of pinking shears. I would have, if it hadn't been for Rosalind."

I drag the note from my pocket and place it on the table between us. "You're saying that my mother, this toxic-to-pets woman, rescued you?"

"Of course, I did." My mother glides into the room wearing a green Dior cocktail dress. Sitting on the sofa she props her rhinestone-encrusted evening slippers besides Clementine's boots. "Did you bring dinner? I'm starved."

I'm not going to correct her about the time; I'm just

grateful she's left behind the doll, she's dressed herself and she's hungry.

Clementine hands her a biscuit and she says, "Did you pin the tail on the donkey?"

Just when my throat is closing over Mother's quick slide into fantasy, Clementine says, "I'm getting to that part."

Nodding like a sage Buddha, Mother stares at the biscuit as if it's an invention requiring an instruction book. Although I'm not hungry, I reach for another biscuit and make a big to-do of eating so she has time to watch and imitate me.

Clementine smiles at me, understanding. "I guess this is a heart to heart, after all."

It's all the praise I'm going to get, but it's enough. I smile back, and she picks up the story where she left off.

"Rosalind knew I was going to self-destruct, so she left her vacation with Jack on Diamond Head and moved in with me, and her pregnant. She also knew I'd never get over it without a huge, cathartic moment."

"I knew." Mother flashes a brilliant smile at us, and I am struck by how little it takes now to make her happy.

All my life I've settled for quiet corners and small moments while she sought center stage and apocalyptic events. I couldn't have handled her grandiosity combined with Alzheimer's. I believe this tamer version of my mother is one of the many tender mercies the Universe hands us when life brings us to our knees.

Thank you, I say. Just that. *Thank you*.

"Rosalind hatched a plan."

Mother giggles. "Like a chicken."

"Disguised in wigs and floppy brimmed hats, we drove to the house where Jerry was propagating with that Jezebel and proceeded to pin donkey tails on all the trees. And above every one we tacked eight by ten glossies of Jerry George."

"The cops were nice."

"Only because of you." She grabs Mother's hand and holds on. "When we got caught Rosalind pretended she was going into labor, so instead of hauling us off to the station they escorted us to the emergency room where she had two doctors and a male nurse swooning at her feet."

Clementine shoots me a black-eyed stare that would make me squirm if I didn't know her.

"Now. Don't you have a job to find?"

"I can't leave you with all this."

"It's not your decision."

I drive straight to the offices of the *Daily Journal*, picturing how I'll present my credentials and the editor will collapse at my feet in gratitude, sobbing, *you're a godsend, an answer to our prayers*.

I ought to write fiction.

What actually happens is that I don't even get past the reception desk. "We're not hiring right now," she says. "You can fill out an application and leave it with us."

After I leave there I head to the mall at Barnes Crossing armed with the help wanted section of the paper. Another hour and four more rejections later I'm convinced everybody in this city has a B.A., a B.S., a Ph.D. or an M.B.A. Everybody except me.

Deciding to console myself with ice cream, I stop at Baskin-Robbins then call Clementine to find out what kind she and Mother want.

"Two chocolates. You'd better bring one for the baby, too."

"She has that doll again?"

"She's rocking it to sleep even as we speak."

In the background I hear singing. In French, if I'm not mistaken. The surprise of Mother is endless. She's a vivid Sun Sprite rose, and every day I discover another layer of petals.

"Ask her what kind of ice cream Sara wants."

"She said peach. I'm proud of you, baby girl."

"I didn't get a job."

"I said I'm proud of you, and I'm sticking to it. Hurry home with that ice cream before it melts."

Outside I'm struggling with the floppy cardboard tray and my pickup door when Officer Mick Hogan strolls up and opens it for me.

"Where did you come from?"

"I saw your truck." He eyes the ice cream. "Looks like you've got company."

Maybe it's his kind face or his blue eyes or the way he helped me get Mother back to bed last night or the fact that he deliberately pulled over at the sight of my Dodge Ram Charger... Whatever the reason, I tell him about the doll waiting for ice cream.

"Sometime, when you can get away, call me. I'll take you down to the racetrack when it's not being used and you can go as fast as you want."

Up to this point, the most romantic gift I've ever received was a box of Valentine's chocolates, the cheap kind without nuts in the center. And that was only because Billy Joe wanted me to run off with him. After we married, romance took a flying leap.

Now here is this man who has done nothing more than share a cup of coffee with me, and yet I feel as if he understands me better than anybody else in the world. Except maybe Clementine.

"Thanks," I tell him. "I definitely will."

When I drive off I don't have the least inclination to speed. I took flight in front of Baskin-Robbins with my feet firmly on the ground.

I GO TO BED that night with the feeling that I'm still flying. Startled awake at 2:00 a.m., I race to check on

Mother. She's sleeping, but a note and her silver pen are on her bedside table.

"Clementine married that scoundrel on the rebound. She loved your father, but he loved me. I have never loved another man. After Jack's plane went down, I kept thinking maybe he survived, maybe he floated ashore somewhere and was waiting for me to find him. I still think that sometimes."

The note ends there. No indecipherable squiggles or confused babbling. Just a sharp punch to the gut that leaves me gasping.

Mother's sleeping peacefully as if she has not been pulled awake in the middle of the night by a mind rising out of darkness and an urgency to translate her history, to build a bridge we can cross while there's still time.

I want to shake her awake, to demand the whole story, but that's a foolish fancy. If I wake her, she's likely to think I'm the Queen of England.

Tiptoeing across the hall, I pull the sheets under my chin and start to see myself and my mother in a new way: I am the child of a couple whose passion was so great Mother spent forty-one years searching for my father, whose love was so fierce that even death and Alzheimer's cannot separate them.

Mother has lived large. She's lived wide awake and wide open. If I pay attention, what I can learn from her is incalculable.

Beloved teacher, Miss Hettie McKenzie, died peacefully in her sleep at the age of 99. Before she passed on, she said what so many others have. "There're two things I want folks to know—every day hug somebody then go out and live as if it's your last hoorah.
From the Obituary of Miss Hettie McKenzie

CHAPTER 7

When Clementine arrives the next morning, I hand her Mother's notes.

She looks up from the last note and says, "I did love Jack. We both met him at a Christmas party. I was instantly and hopelessly smitten, but he had eyes only for Rosalind. I was a bridesmaid at the wedding."

"Didn't that hurt? Why would Mother put you through that?"

"A friendship like ours can't be reduced to a simple explanation."

"I want to know about the other notes, especially the tree. Why would she say love is like a tree, ask Clementine?"

"I'll tell you one more thing and then I want you to get out of here and look for work. Rosalind and Jack included me in every aspect of their marriage except the bedroom. I couldn't have felt more cherished if I had married him, myself."

Little Bit barks and I hear Mother tapping our way, probably wearing her high-heeled mules with feather trim.

"Who stole my ballet slippers?"

"Scoot, Sara. I'll take care of this."

IT'S NOT WORK I'm thinking about as I drive off, but forty years of missing my mother, of waking to the whirr of Clementine's sewing machine and wishing it were another sound, Mother in the kitchen singing along with the radio or in the shower singing above the roar of water.

I don't know whether her singing is a distant memory I recall or whether it's a fantasy fueled by her recent renditions of opera in French and Italian.

Which leads to the question of her fluency in foreign languages. And her fascination with all musical forms. Dance, for instance. Why does she keep asking for ballet slippers?

I feel like a woman piecing together a patchwork quilt of her life, one square at a time. The irony is that just as I'm finding the pieces, Mother is losing them.

Seized with sudden inspiration, I abandon my job hunt in search of an album. If I dig up bits of her past and glue them inside—airline ticket stubs, old opera programs, faded photographs, my birth certificate, her marriage license—

perhaps the pages will anchor her to reality, tether her wandering mind a while longer.

Long enough for me to find her again.

Please, God.

I shift directions toward Wal-Mart, and as I turn onto Main Street the sign in the window of *The Courier* leaps out at me. "Society editor wanted."

"Divine intervention."

Call me a starry-eyed mystic, but I believe in signs. Miracles, even. When the Universe taps me on the shoulder, I sit up and pay attention. Wal-Mart will have to wait.

The Courier has bells on the front door. Another good sign.

I walk inside and transform myself from a wallflower into a potential social maven, mingling with lively people who sponsor benefit concerts, throw lavish wedding receptions and call to invite you to holiday extravaganzas.

Not only do I get to reinvent myself, but I also get to stay home part time with Mother. This is a weekly paper, a small staff, a nice boss. Virginia Cooper.

When I tell her about Mother, she says, "Don't worry. Around here, families come first."

Now Clementine can rescue Mother and still have time to putter in her garden and make beautiful dresses at her sewing machine and prop her cowboy boots on the footrest of her recliner and take a nap.

WHEN I RETURN HOME they are playing checkers. I say this very loosely because Mother's not playing by any rules I ever heard of, but she's laughing. And that's all that counts.

"You're looking at Tupelo's newest society editor."

"I knew you could do it," Clementine says while Mother says, "Let's go to Paris. Jack's there."

I think there's a travel magazine around here with pictures of Paris's major attractions I can cut and paste in the album along with photos of Daddy.

"Tonight we'll dress up and see the Eiffel Tower."

Mother claps her hands and Clementine nods her approval even though she knows nothing about the album.

"Do you want to take my place at the game board, Sara?" Clementine rises stiffly, lines of fatigue etched around her eyes. "It's time to see the tree. If Rosalind is up to it, we'll go tomorrow."

"Let's wait a few days. I don't report to work until next Monday. Stay home and rest."

"You might need me tomorrow."

"I need you the rest of my life, Clementine, but I need you alive and not half dead."

"It'll take more than making a sandwich and sitting on my butt playing checkers to kill me."

She hangs a big straw purse on her arm, beige raffia woven with brightly colored raffia flowers. If it's not the same one I remember from my childhood, it's the exact twin. The straw bag always contained Clementine's latest sewing project, a box of cookies, several chocolate bars, a bottle of water and whatever books and small toys I happened to favor at the time. I always imagined that if I ever ran away, all I'd need was Clementine's purse.

It's funny how something as insignificant as a purse can trigger memories of childhood. And home.

Now I understand that she carried more than possessions in her purse: she carried food and laughter and comfort. Our lives lay inside the raffia depths, intertwined. Waiting at the airport for Mother's plane, we shared a candy bar. Sitting in hard chairs at the doctor's office, I read *Sleeping Beauty* while she read *The Sound and the Fury*. With my legs dangling from the child's seat in the grocery store cart, I dug into the purse for my blue velvet rabbit and chocolate chip cookie.

Now I tell Clementine, "Tomorrow I want to see the tree." Tomorrow I want to add the centerpiece to the patchwork quilt of my life.

"Call me when Rosalind is up and ready to go."

LATER THAT EVENING, sitting together on the sofa dressed in gloves and hats unearthed from a cedar chest stamped with Rosalind Ryan's name, Mother traces pictures of the Eiffel Tower and Daddy in his pilot's uniform. Suddenly she starts singing "La Vie en Rose."

"Will you teach that song to me?"

"Who are you?"

"Somebody who loves you."

"Oh, all right then. You can sing, too."

I leave my world behind and enter hers, a drab woman turned interesting and mysterious, singing in French.

MOTHER AND I have the kind of morning that makes me wonder if I have the courage, strength, stamina and wisdom to handle the physical upheaval and emotional turmoil of this long goodbye.

In contrast to last night's quiet evening with the album and French songs, today everything we do—bathe, dress, eat breakfast—is a small struggle. Everything we accomplish, a small victory.

By ten o'clock I'm exhausted. I almost call Clementine and tell her not to come, but I don't want to disappoint her. And in spite of the morning's turmoil, Mother's happy.

"I've packed a picnic," Clementine says. "And I'm coming in Rosalind's car."

"Will that upset her?"

"I don't think so. I think she'll be excited."

Clementine's right. Mother's so excited she wants to drive. It takes an act of congress (Clementine saying, "Over my dead body,") and an act of God (Mother nearly tipping over and spraining her ankle in the ridiculous sling-back heels she insisted on wearing) to change her mind.

After I've found Ace bandages in the medicine cabinet and wrapped her ankle, I climb behind the wheel and follow Clementine's directions to the Natchez Trace Parkway.

"How far?"

"Just keep going south till I tell you to stop."

She doesn't say stop until we come to a scenic site called Witch Dance. The legend on the sign says this is a place where witches once danced, and everywhere their feet touched no grass grows.

I park underneath the shade of an ancient black jack oak, and the reverent silence of green forest and deep blue sky overcomes us. We sit in the car, three women connected by heartstrings and a tree that lies somewhere in the primeval depths of the woods.

"I know this place." Mother looks at me with clear eyes, then glances at her feet. "Why am I wearing high heels?"

From the back seat Clementine says, "Pull them off. You're liable to break your neck. On top of everything else."

"I'm sorry, Sara." Mother reaches over and holds my hand. "For everything."

This is one of those rare moments when she's fully with me. I could ask her dozens of important questions: Why did you leave me? Why didn't you take me along? Didn't you know I needed you?

"Mother, why do you keep asking for ballet shoes?"

"I was going to study dance."

"She gave up scholarships in New York and a chance to be a famous ballerina for you and Jack."

"You were pregnant when you married my father?"

"Yes, but I would have married him anyway."

"Are we going to sit in this car all day getting maudlin?" Clementine opens her door and bails out, followed by Mother in stocking feet. "Good Lord, Rosalind. I don't know why I didn't make you change shoes before we left."

"Here," I say. "We'll swap."

Now I'm walking in my mother's shoes, finding out what it's like to think you'll fall but plunging boldly forward anyhow.

It's funny how a pair of strappy red high heels can make you feel feminine and alluring. Maybe I'll borrow some of Mother's shoes, wear them on my new job. Get some cute skirts. Learn to cross my legs and let one shoe dangle from the toe.

"What are you giggling about?" Clementine says.

"Life."

"I'm going to have to find something to call you besides baby girl. Looks like you've grown up on me."

"I can't seem to find my purse."

"You didn't bring a purse, Rosalind."

Mother's drifting off again. But when I assure her she doesn't need one, we'll take care of her, she smiles in a way that lets me know she's still in there somewhere. Beneath the confusion lie her spirit and her soul, her personality and her life's experiences. Beneath the fog of this heartbreaking illness is still Rosalind Ryan.

Clementine and I hold her firmly between us, matching our pace to hers, stopping when she wants to admire a tiny purple wood violet, a red-headed woodpecker tapping at a Tupelo gum tree, a lizard slithering across our path.

The tree is in a cathedral-like clearing, a large oak with the carving still clearly visible. While Clementine spreads a quilt, I put my hands inside the carved-out heart, trace the three names: Rosalind, Clementine, Sara.

"When she found out she was pregnant, Rosalind was scared to death." Clementine gently urges Mother to the quilt, then sits beside her, holding her hand. "She knew something was missing in her. Maybe it was the nesting instinct. I don't know."

I sit beside them on the quilt, take hold of Mother's other hand and don't let go.

"Rosalind came to me and said, 'If I tell Jack I don't know how to be a mother, he'll hate me. I can't bear that.' I told her I would be there with her. Her baby would be mine. Lord, little did we know."

I fill in the blanks. That Clementine couldn't have children. That Jack would die. That Rosalind would fly away.

"After you were born we came here and carved this tree. Rosalind believed in rituals. She picked the place. 'If I had chosen dance, my life would have been barren, no grass would have grown.' That heart with our three names was our secret pact that the three of us would always be bound together."

I reach for Clementine's hand, joining the three of us in a circle.

Now I understand. When Mother flew to Paris or London or Milan, she didn't abandon me: she gave me the best mother a little girl could have, the best mother a grown woman reinventing herself and piecing together Rosalind Ryan can have.

The tree will endure and so will we. I see us going into the future bound together by love, lifting each other up when one of us falls and crying together when one of us hurts. But most of all I see us laughing over everything from singing French songs to dancing in ballet slippers with Mother to roaring around the racetrack with a certain red-haired Irishman who knows how to banish loneliness and make a woman believe in her own power.

Mediterranean Nights

Join the guests and crew of Alexandra's Dream,
the newest luxury ship to set sail on the
romantic Mediterranean, as they experience
the glamorous world of cruising.

A new Harlequin continuity series
begins in June 2007 with
FROM RUSSIA, WITH LOVE
by Ingrid Weaver

Marina Artamova books a cabin on the luxurious
cruise ship Alexandra's Dream, when she finds out that
her orphaned nephew and his adoptive father are aboard.
She's determined to be reunited with the boy…but
the romantic ambience of the ship and her undeniable
attraction to a man she considers her enemy
are about to interfere with her quest!

Turn the page for a sneak preview!

Piraeus, Greece

"There she is, Stefan. *Alexandra's Dream.*" David Anderson squatted beside his new son and pointed at the dark blue hull that towered above the pier. The cruise ship was a majestic sight, twelve decks high and as long as a city block. A circle of silver and gold stars, the logo of the Liberty Cruise Line, gleamed from the swept-back smokestack. Like some legendary sea creature born for the water, the ship emanated power from every sleek curve—even at rest it held the promise of motion. "That's going to be our home for the next ten days."

The child beside him remained silent, his cheeks working in and out as he sucked furiously on his thumb. Hair so blond it appeared white ruffled against his forehead in the harbor breeze. The baby-sweet scent unique to the very young mingled with the tang of the sea.

"Ship," David said. "Uh, *parakhod.*"

From beneath his bangs, Stefan looked at the *Alexandra's*

Dream. Although he didn't release his thumb, the corners of his mouth tightened with the beginning of a smile.

David grinned. That was Stefan's first smile this afternoon, one of only two since they had left the orphanage yesterday. It was probably because of the boat—according to the orphanage staff, the boy loved boats, which was the main reason David had decided to book this cruise. Then again, there was a strong possibility the smile could have been a reaction to David's attempt at pocket-dictionary Russian. Whatever the cause, it was a good start.

The liaison from the adoption agency had claimed that Stefan had been taught some English, but David had yet to see evidence of it. David continued to speak, positive his son would understand his tone even if he couldn't grasp the words. "This is her maiden voyage. Her first trip, just like this is our first trip, and that makes it special." He motioned toward the stage that had been set up on the pier beneath the ship's bow. "That's why everyone's celebrating."

The ship's official christening ceremony had been held the day before and had been a closed affair, with only the cruise-line executives and VIP guests invited, but the stage hadn't yet been disassembled. Banners bearing the blue and white of the Greek flag of the ship's owner, as well as the Liberty circle of stars logo, draped the edges of the platform. In the center, a group of musicians and a dance troupe dressed in tra-

ditional white folk costumes performed for the benefit of the
Alexandra's Dream's first passengers. Their audience was in a
festive mood, snapping their fingers in time to the music
while the dancers twirled and wove through their steps.

David bobbed his head to the rhythm of the mandolins.
They were playing a folk tune that seemed vaguely familiar,
possibly from a movie he'd seen. He hummed a few notes.
"Catchy melody, isn't it?"

Stefan turned his gaze on David. His eyes were a striking
shade of blue, as cool and pale as a winter horizon and far
too solemn for a child not yet five. Still, the smile that
hovered at the corners of his mouth persisted. He moved his
head with the music, mirroring David's motion.

David gave a silent cheer at the interaction. Hopefully,
this cruise would provide countless opportunities for more.
"Hey, good for you," he said. "Do you like the music?"

The child's eyes sparked. He withdrew his thumb with a
pop. *"Moozika!"*

"Music. Right!" David held out his hand. "Come on,
let's go closer so we can watch the dancers."

Stefan grasped David's hand quickly, as if he feared it
would be withdrawn. In an instant his budding smile was
replaced by a look close to panic.

Did he remember the car accident that had killed his
parents? It would be a mercy if he didn't. As far as David knew,
Stefan had never spoken of it to anyone. Whatever he had

seen had made him run so far from the crash that the police hadn't found him until the next day. The event had traumatized him to the extent that he hadn't uttered a word until his fifth week at the orphanage. Even now he seldom talked.

David sat back on his heels and brushed the hair from Stefan's forehead. That solemn, too-old gaze locked with his, and for an instant, David felt as if he looked back in time at an image of himself thirty years ago.

He didn't need to speak the same language to understand exactly how this boy felt. He knew what it meant to be alone and powerless among strangers, trying to be brave and tough but wishing with every fiber of his being for a place to belong, to be safe, and most of all for someone to love him....

He knew in his heart he would be a good parent to Stefan. It was why he had never considered halting the adoption process after Ellie had left him. He hadn't balked when he'd learned of the recent claim by Stefan's spinster aunt, either; the absentee relative had shown up too late for her case to be considered. The adoption was meant to be. He and this child already shared a bond that went deeper than paperwork or legalities.

A seagull screeched overhead, making Stefan start and press closer to David.

"That's my boy," David murmured. He swallowed hard, struck by the simple truth of what he had just said.

That's my boy.

"I CAN'T BE PATIENT, RUDOLPH. I'm not going to stand by and watch my nephew get ripped from his country and his roots to live on the other side of the world."

Rudolph hissed out a slow breath. "Marina, I don't like the sound of that. What are you planning?"

"I'm going to talk some sense into this American kidnapper."

"No. Absolutely not. No offence, but diplomacy is not your strong suit."

"Diplomacy be damned. Their ship's due to sail at five o'clock."

"Then you wouldn't have an opportunity to speak with him even if his lawyer agreed to a meeting."

"I'll have ten days of opportunities, Rudolph, since I plan to be on board that ship."

* * * * *

Follow Marina and David as they join forces to uncover the reason behind little Stefan's unusual silence, and the secret behind the death of his parents....

Look for
From Russia, With Love
by Ingrid Weaver
in stores June 2007.

Romantic
SUSPENSE

**Sparked by Danger,
Fueled by Passion.**

*This month and every month look for
four new heart-racing romances
set against a backdrop of suspense!*

Available in June 2007

Shelter from the Storm
by RaeAnne Thayne

A Little Bit Guilty
(Midnight Secrets miniseries)
by Jenna Mills

Mob Mistress
by Sheri WhiteFeather

A Serial Affair
by Natalie Dunbar

Available wherever you buy books!

Visit Silhouette Books at www.eHarlequin.com   SRS0507

HARLEQUIN®
SuperRomance®

Acclaimed author
Brenda Novak
returns to Dundee, Idaho, with

COULDA BEEN A COWBOY

After gaining custody of his infant son,
professional athlete Tyson Garnier hopes to escape
the media and find some privacy in Dundee, Idaho.
He also finds Dakota Brown. But is she ready for the
potential drama that comes with him?

Also watch for:

BLAME IT ON THE DOG by Amy Frazier
(Singles...with Kids)

HIS PERFECT WOMAN by Kay Stockham

DAD FOR LIFE by Helen Brenna
(A Little Secret)

MR. IRRESISTIBLE by Karina Bliss

WANTED MAN by Ellen K. Hartman

Available June 2007 wherever Harlequin books are sold!

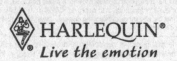

HARLEQUIN®
Live the emotion

www.eHarlequin.com   HSR0507

REQUEST YOUR FREE BOOKS!

2 FREE NOVELS PLUS 2 FREE GIFTS!

There's the life you planned. And there's what comes next.

YES! Please send me 2 FREE Harlequin® NEXT™ novels and my 2 FREE mystery gifts. After receiving them, if I don't wish to receive any more books, I can return the shipping statement marked "cancel." If I don't cancel, I will receive 4 brand-new novels every other month and be billed just $3.99 per book in the U.S. or $4.74 per book in Canada, plus 25¢ shipping and handling per book plus applicable taxes, if any.* That's a savings of over 25% off the cover price! I understand that accepting the 2 free books and gifts places me under no obligation to buy anything. I can always return a shipment and cancel at any time. Even if I never buy anything from Harlequin, the two free books and gifts are mine to keep forever.   155 HDN EL33 355 HDN EL4F

Name _____ (PLEASE PRINT) _____

Address _____ Apt. # _____

City _____ State/Prov. _____ Zip/Postal Code _____

Signature (if under 18, a parent or guardian must sign)

Order online at www.TryNEXTNovels.com

Or mail to the **Harlequin Reader Service®**:
IN U.S.A.: P.O. Box 1867, Buffalo, NY 14240-1867
IN CANADA: P.O. Box 609, Fort Erie, Ontario L2A 5X3

Not valid to current Harlequin NEXT subscribers.

Want to try two free books from another line?
Call 1-800-873-8635 or visit www.morefreebooks.com

* Terms and prices subject to change without notice. NY residents add applicable sales tax. Canadian residents will be charged applicable provincial taxes and GST. This offer is limited to one order per household. All orders subject to approval. Credit or debit balances in a customer's account(s) may be offset by any other outstanding balance owed by or to the customer. Please allow 4 to 6 weeks for delivery.

Your Privacy: Harlequin Books is committed to protecting your privacy. Our Privacy Policy is available online at www.eHarlequin.com or upon request from the Harlequin Reader Service. From time to time we make our lists of customers available to reputable firms who may have a product or service of interest to you. If you would prefer we not share your name and address, please check here. ☐

NEXT07R

SPECIAL EDITION™

COMING IN JUNE

HER LAST FIRST DATE

by *USA TODAY* bestselling author
SUSAN MALLERY

After one too many bad dates, Crissy Phillips
finally swore off men. Recently widowed,
pediatrician Josh Daniels can't risk losing his
heart. With an intense attraction pulling them
together, will their fear keep them apart?
Or will one wild night change everything...?

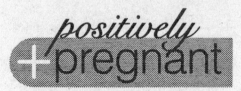

Sometimes the unexpected is the best news of all....

Visit Silhouette Books at www.eHarlequin.com   SSE24831

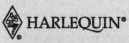

COMING NEXT MONTH

#85 PRIME TIME • Hank Phillippi Ryan
In her debut novel, real-life Boston TV reporter
Hank Phillippi Ryan takes you behind the scenes of TV
news—its on-camera glitz and off-camera grit. *Prime Time*'s
heroine, Charlie McNally, is investigating the scoop of her
career—one that could lead to the man of her dreams...or
get her killed for knowing way, *way* too much.

#86 MADAM OF THE HOUSE • Donna Birdsell
With sales in the toilet and her soon-to-be-ex sucking her
savings dry, real estate agent Cecilia Katz and her handsome
assistant devise a very *special* open house—charging single
friends of a certain age to hook up with young men in need
of cold, hard cash. Can the makeshift madam close the
deal...or will this risky business be her downfall?